"Anne, you're going to have a new sister-in-law. What do you think of that?"

The girl turned her head slowly as if her neck were stiff and gave him a small secret smile. "I think I'm going to kill her," she said.

These Cliffs Are Dangerous

LINDSAY MARCH

A FAWCETT CREST BOOK

Fawcett Publications, Inc., Greenwich, Conn.

THESE CLIFFS ARE DANGEROUS

A Fawcett Crest Book reprinted by arrangement with
Simon and Schuster

Library of Congress Catalog Card Number: 72-90397

Printed in the United States of America

First printing: January 1975

1 2 3 4 5 6 7 8 9 10

1

ONE

The Strattons had begun to give their weird parties less than a year before Harlan's death. At least, Jenny had thought the parties weird, but, as Harlan had constantly reminded her, she was a stranger to New York and what might seem weird to her was unremarkable when placed against the background of that glittering urban nightmare. The Strattons' parties, however, had been far from unremarkable. "Sophisticated," Harlan had called them, and later, having acquired some of the Strattons' trans-Atlantic slang: "Quite unbelievably Now, darling."

Jenny often wondered what had happened to Guy and Christina Stratton.

Even now, six months after Harlan's death, she could still blame the Strattons for the car accident which had taken his life. She knew this was foolish, for the Strattons had left New York and returned to London long before Harlan had been killed, but it was the Strattons who had changed Harlan, the Strattons who had sent him on the feverish pursuit of the unbelievable Now, the Strattons who had liberated Harlan from the traditional values instilled into him by his rigidly traditional family.

"My dear Jenny," Guy Stratton had said to her at one of those never-ending parties, "all children rebel against their parents sooner or later. Harlan simply did it later than most children, that's all."

Whatever could have happened to Guy Stratton?

She could still see him so clearly, tall, lean and much too good-looking, his dark eyes regarding her with that casual amusement which she had found both repellent and fascinating. What could it be like to be married to a man as attractive as that? It had been hard enough being married to Harlan, and Harlan with his boyish enthusiasm and good-natured naiveté had been simplicity itself compared with a man like Guy Stratton.

"Darling," Guy's wife Christina had said to her once, "Harlan's such a poppet. All that dreadful money in his family hasn't spoiled him at all."

That had been true enough; the wealthy family with their Quaker heritage hadn't spoiled Harlan. The Strattons were the ones who had changed him for the worse.

"Live a little, Harlan," Guy had said. "Nobody's going to reach down from heaven and strike you dead."

But he had died.

He had driven his red Porsche into the back of a truck on the Connecticut Turnpike and killed both himself and his passenger. Jenny had hardly known the dead girl. Harlan had met her at the Strattons' and later, in an attempt to live up to his playboy image—the image the Strattons had created for him—had decided to demonstrate his skill with fast cars to this blonde model who had caught his fancy. But his skill had been no match for the wet road and the mist which had hidden the heavy truck until too late.

Harlan's family were polite to her at the funeral, but no

more than polite. She knew they blamed her for being an indirect cause of his death. If he had not incurred the family's disapproval by marrying her, he would have stayed in Boston and not ventured into the brash wasteland of New York. New York had changed him, and who was responsible for sending him to New York?

Useless to try to explain to them about the Strattons.

At that disastrous last party a year ago, Guy had said, "You know, Jenny, in your shy, quiet little way, you're really rather attractive. I think I'd like to go to bed with you." And later in the corridor as she was trying to escape: "Well, naturally you feel the odd one out when you won't join in the fun! If you'd try it just once—wonderful aphrodisiac—forget all those old-fashioned inhibitions of yours. . . ."

"But you *are* so old-fashioned, Jenny!" Harlan had said, irritated, afterwards. "Do you really have to be so damn square all the time? So what if Guy did make a pass at you? At least he was reacting in a real, honest way. He wanted to reach out and be close to you—can't you see? He wanted to make a gesture of love. Well, I think that's beautiful. After all, love *is* beautiful. Love is—"

"You don't know one damn thing about love!" she had blazed, shocking herself even more than him by losing a temper she had barely known she possessed. "Not one damn thing! All you know about is phony talk, phony dreams and getting stoned!"

They hadn't spoken to each other for three days after that, and by the time they were speaking to each other again the Strattons had gone. Guy's father had died; Guy had had to return to England for the funeral, and while he was in London his boss had decided to recall him permanently from New York. Personnel from the New York office of that famous firm of architects had arranged to sublease the apartment, sell the Lincoln Continental and ship back the Strattons' furniture, clothing and personal possessions.

Life went on. New people—dull people, Harlan had soon decided—had moved into the Strattons' apartment next door, but the Strattons' friends were still giving parties. The curious part was that nobody had ever heard from the Strattons after their return to England; Jenny had not even heard from them when Harlan died, and that had surprised her, for Harlan had prided himself on being such a close friend of Guy's and in the early days, at least, Christina had taken Jenny "under her wing," as he had phrased it. They had gone shopping together at Bergdorf Goodman, Christina had told her what to buy and Jenny had listened gratefully because Christina at twenty-nine was immeasurably more chic than Jenny at nineteen, from a quiet London suburb, could ever hope to be.

But Christina had never written, although she and Guy must have been aware of Harlan's death. The flamboyant and violent end of one of America's youngest multimillionaires had had enough publicity in the American press to merit a paragraph in the British dailies; Jenny's father had written with gloomy pride to tell her that the incident had been mentioned in the America column of the *Daily Express*.

To her distress, Jenny found that her memory of the Strattons seemed to grow clearer, not dimmer, during the months after Harlan's death. Eventually she decided that this was because she was giving herself too much time to think about them; it was foolish—and bad for her—to sit around passively in her new apartment or go shopping on

Fifth Avenue to pass the afternoons, and the sooner she decided to do something constructive with her time the better. Despite the fact that she now had more money than she would ever need, she knew it would be better for her to have a job. But that raised the question of whether she wanted to continue living in New York or return to England. She had always planned to visit her father and stepmother one day, but a visit was very different from an indefinite stay, particularly since she had lost contact with her former friends in London. At least in New York she knew some young people and at last was beginning to feel at home.

Time passed, yet she came no closer to reaching a decision. One fine spring afternoon she tried again to make up her mind, but when she failed she went outside restlessly and headed crosstown toward Fifth Avenue. Anything, even another aimless shopping expedition, was better than sitting indoors worrying about the future. She was just wandering dreamily past a window where diamonds languished on black velvet, when the great doors of Tiffany's revolved and out walked Guy Stratton.

TWO

The shock of seeing him again was so intense that she did not at first notice how much he had changed. He wore dark glasses, and because part of his face was hidden she was surprised that she should recognize him so quickly. He was thinner; the skin was stretched more tightly across the bones of his face, and there was a narrower set to his mouth. He wore a lightweight gray suit and his dark-blue tie was somber against his white shirt.

For some reason she was convinced he would not recognize her, and so when he stopped dead and said, "Jenny!" in an astonished voice, she found herself tongue-tied with a mixture of gratification, shyness and—remembering their disastrous last encounter—embarrassment.

"It *is Jenny,* isn't it?" he said. "Jenny Dexter?"

"Yes—what a surprise to see you again!" The words tumbled out unevenly. "I didn't think—I didn't know you were back in New York."

"It's just a business trip. I'm going home at the weekend."

"Oh."

There was a pause. Traffic roared past them down the avenue. The acrid reek of diesel fumes mingled with the dust and dirt of the busy sidewalk.

Unnerved by his silence she heard herself say clumsily, "You've been shopping at Tiffany's?"

"I bought a small present for my sister."

"Your sister? Oh yes, I remember your mentioning her. She's a lot younger than you, isn't she, and was away at finishing school in Switzerland." Cocktail party conversation, she thought. Bright, empty, meaningless.

There was another pause. She could not understand why Guy should be so silent, for one of the things she remembered best about him was his gift for putting people at ease with his ready conversation and effortless charm. Perhaps he was even more embarrassed than she was by the meeting. Perhaps he was sorry he had recognized her and was now anxious to escape. Frantically she searched for a rapid way of terminating the encounter and then remembered that it would seem odd indeed if she rushed away without inquiring politely after his wife.

"And how's Christina?" she said in a rush. "Do remember me to her when you go home, won't you? I hope she's well."

It was not until then that he took off his sunglasses. Without them his eyes seemed darker than she remembered, and suddenly, intuitively, she knew what he was going to say and felt her heart thump against her ribs.

"Christina died," he said. "It was nearly a year ago now, soon after we went back to England. It was an accident."

"But how dreadful—I—I'm so sorry. I didn't know—"

"No, why should you have known? You're not one of the expatriates who make a hobby of reading the obituary columns of the English newspapers. I didn't expect you to know."

"No, but—"

"I was in a different position," he said. "I read about Harlan. I should have written but I didn't. I'm sorry."

"That's all right. . . . I didn't expect—"

"No, I don't suppose you did, but I should still have written. But maybe I thought you'd prefer not to be reminded of my existence."

"You needn't have thought that."

"No? Look, I'm sorry about what happened at that last party. I always meant to apologize but when my father died and we had to leave New York so suddenly there was simply no opportunity to see you again."

"Yes, of course. I quite understand."

"I wonder if you do," he said. He stood there looking down at her, and suddenly the tension ebbed from his face as he smiled. "Would you forgive me enough to accept an invitation to dinner?"

"Well . . ." She could not believe that he was really

anxious to dine with her. "I'm sure you must be very busy since your time here's so short—there must be so many of your old friends that you want to see—"

"You're quite wrong," he said. "I haven't seen any of them. And of all the people I used to know in New York you're the only one I'd care to exchange more than half a dozen words with. However, if you'd prefer to steer clear of me after our last meeting—"

"Oh, it's not that!"

"Then let me call for you at . . . let's say six-thirty, and we can have a quiet dinner somewhere."

"That's . . . very nice of you. Thank you."

"Are you still at the same apartment?"

"No, I moved." She told him her new address and he wrote it down on the back of an envelope.

"Till six-thirty then," he said, slipping both envelope and pen back into his pocket. "I'll be looking forward to it."

"Six-thirty," she repeated, mesmerized, and watched him walk away from her until he was lost from sight in the crowds.

THREE

When she saw him again four hours later he seemed more like the Guy she remembered, more relaxed, more talk-ative, more casual, and she wondered if her earlier im-pression of change had been an illusion created by the surprise of their meeting.

"What will you drink?" said Guy as they settled down

at their table and the waiters began to flutter around them like moths. "Are whiskey sours still in favor?"

"Heavens, what a memory!" And then she recalled that Harlan had complained to her once in Guy's presence that whiskey sours were unadventurous and she should try something else.

Guy was saying to the waiter, "One whiskey sour, please, and one martini, straight up, with an olive." As he spoke he opened a new packet of cigarettes and held it out to her. "Smoke?"

"Thanks." She took one and had accepted a light before she realized that he was putting the packet away without taking a cigarette for himself.

"You don't want to smoke?" she said surprised.

"I gave it up." He examined the clean ashtray with clinical interest and did not look at her.

"Completely?" She was impressed.

"Yes, I decided I needed to perform some sort of penance," he said lightly, "and giving up smoking seemed to be the best way to martyr myself."

She wanted to ask why a penance had seemed necessary, but she had no wish to seem inquisitive so she merely smiled. She was still smiling when he looked up at her swiftly across the table and said in that same light casual voice, "I had more success than I thought I would. I don't smoke anything now."

Around them the restaurant hummed and glowed with quiet life, a party of six was being seated at a table across the room; nearby a waiter was busily preparing crepes suzette over a flame.

"Well, enough of my tedious tales of abstinence and

self-denial," said Guy. "Let's talk of something else. Is it really true that life in New York has become even more frenetic during the past year? I hear one has to be a millionaire nowadays before one can rent a decent apartment in Manhattan."

"Yes, it *is* awful how things have gone up." As the waiter arrived with their drinks she told Guy of the struggle she had had to find a new apartment after Harlan's death. "I'm lucky that I don't have to worry about money," she said frankly. "How people less fortunate manage I just don't know."

"Harlan left you all right financially, did he? The money didn't revert to that straitlaced family under some antiquated trust?"

"Some of it did. But even so I'm still more than well provided for."

"That's lucky." He took a large sip of his drink. "What do you do with yourself these days when you're not pacing the New York pavements in search of an apartment?"

She told him of her tentative plans to take a business course, and they spent several minutes discussing the kind of job which would suit her best. Finally after a long and unexpectedly serious review of the city's employment opportunities for young widows with secretarial skills, Guy said, "Why don't you come back to England and work in London?"

"Oh . . ." She sighed. "Reasons . . . It's difficult."

"What's the problem? No wait a minute, I think I can remember. Didn't you come to America originally to escape from your family? There was a wicked stepmother, wasn't there, and a father who took umbrage when you told him there were more interesting things in life than selling biscuits in his grocer's shop. Told you that you owed him something and didn't think much of your very adventurous gesture of going to America to work as an *au pair*."

"Poor Dad!" Jenny sighed a second time. "Of course he was right—I did owe him something, but—"

"Oh, that old argument! My father used the same line, if that's any consolation. 'Oh Guy,' he used to say, 'my fondest dreams would be realized if you became a solicitor and went into the family firm—and you do owe it to me, you know, after all I've done for you.' Well, perhaps he didn't put it as blatantly as that, but he was certainly very offended when his fondest dreams and mine didn't coincide. Ironically enough I've often thought since that I might have preferred a career in the law. I get very bored sometimes with designing plumbing systems for skyscrapers."

"Successfully designing plumbing systems for skyscrapers."

"That's true," said Guy. "Thank you for reminding me. Yes, my father eventually recovered from his disappointment that I didn't follow in his professional footsteps, and admitted he was pleased that I was doing so well. Not that this long-delayed stamp of approval made much difference to our relationship. We always found it hard to get on with each other, and after he retired from the firm, remarried and went to live in Cellanporth I seldom saw him."

"Had he been retired long when he died?"

"Two years. Christina and I only went down to Cellanporth once while he was alive, but we went there for the funeral and stayed several days. My sister Anne was just home from her finishing school in Switzerland and I hadn't seen her for a long time; then Marguerite—my father's second wife—needed help sorting out my father's papers. Anyway, the firm owed me three weeks' holiday, so I decided to spent it at Cellanporth, much to Christina's disgust. She was annoyed at being dragged away from New York and wanted to console herself by going to the Costa Brava or the Italian Riviera. Still, even in Cellanporth we found a couple of people who would have been quite at home among our New York crowd, so —would you like another drink?"

"Well . . ."

"Another round of the same, please. Yes, we became friendly with these people and there was a party. A lot of people came down from London, and it quickly became obvious that the evening was going to be just as—entertaining as any we'd had in Manhattan." There was a pause. He was very still. "The party ended on the cliffs above the sea," he said slowly. He had picked up his fork and was gripping it hard. "Nobody could remember much about it afterwards, but the next morning Christina was found dead on the beach. The coroner made a great many scathing remarks about wild parties, and the verdict was accidental death." He paused again. "I can't think why I'm telling you all this," he said at last. "Perhaps it's because I sensed you'd want to know what happened. Or perhaps it's because I still think about it a lot, even after almost a year."

"It must have been a dreadful shock for you."

"Yes, it was a shock, but you needn't feel too sorry for me. There's no sense in being hypocritical. Christina and I weren't very happy together. In fact—" He broke off as he saw her expression. "Surely you must have realized that!"

"No, I . . . always thought you were so well-suited."

"Bizarre, unfaithful, but well-suited!"

"One whiskey sour," intoned the waiter behind Jenny's shoulder. "And one martini."

"However," said Guy, "even though it wasn't the best marriage in the world I wouldn't have wanted it to end in that particular way."

"I—"

"Yes?"

"—felt the same way about my marriage, too."

"Would you like to see the menu, sir?" The waiter was fluttering at their elbows again, and they accepted menus obediently.

After they had ordered Jenny said, "During this past year—since Christina died—have you been back to Cellanporth?"

"Yes, often. My sister has been ill. She still is ill, unfortunately, and so I've been visiting her as often as possible."

"I hope it's nothing serious."

"She had a nervous breakdown." He was examining the ashtray again, and she knew instinctively that it was one of those moments when he longed to light a cigarette. "But she's getting better. It's a slow business, that's all." And as if to divert himself, he pushed the ashtray aside, took a long drink of his martini and beckoned the waiter. "The wine list, please."

Jenny eyed her whiskey sour. Since Harlan's death she had fallen out of the habit of having cocktails and was aware that her tolerance for alcohol would be low.

"Jenny—"

It was strange how she had learned more about him in one evening than during all those months when they had been neighbors. He had certainly changed; she was beginning to suspect too that the changes in him were deeper than she had first realized. There was no longer any barrier blocking her unwilling fascination. She saw now with uneasy clarity that part of the hostility she had felt for him in the past had been based on fear—fear because she found him physically more attractive than her own husband, fear because she sensed how easy it would be to fall in love with him, fear because he would be incapable of regarding her as anything more than a source of amusement drifting on the fringes of the bright dangerous world in which he lived.

"Jenny—"

"Yes?"

"You seem different," he said, uncannily echoing her own thoughts, and added with a smile, "You seem—how shall I describe it?—more mature, more sure of yourself. You were such a shy little thing when we first met you. I remember Christina saying—" He stopped.

"Yes?" said Jenny. "What did she say?"

"She said, 'What on earth does he see in her?' But later all I could think was, 'What on earth does she see in him?' Christina thought you married him for all that damned money, but it wasn't that, was it? Harlan meant much more to you than just a blank check."

"Much more," she said wryly, "although no one ever really believed it. But when I first arrived in America I was very lonely and homesick, and although his family were kind to me I was no more than just another servant in their eyes. And then just as I was convinced I'd made an awful mistake, Harlan came home from college. I wasn't just 'the new maid' to him. We talked a lot and found we both laughed at the same things and soon I'd forgotten all about how homesick I'd felt—" She stopped. To her horror she felt tears prick at the back of her eyes. When she tried to speak again all she could say was, "We were so happy. In the beginning."

The cutlery had blurred into the white tablecloth. She was still wondering in panic if she would be able to control her tears when Guy's hand slid across the table to cover hers, and his voice, so clear and English, said gently, "Forgive me. I shouldn't have asked you to talk about him. I forgot it's only been six months since his death."

"It's all right." She had conquered her tears and her voice had a stubborn ring as if she were trying to convince herself as well as him that she had recovered her poise. "It's all over now. It doesn't matter any more." After a moment she was even able to withdraw her hand from his and say calmly, "You're right—I *am* different now, I'm not nineteen any more and I'm not living in a house where I'm treated as a servant and I'm no longer overwhelmed if anyone decides to take some notice of me. I've changed a lot in the two years since I married Harlan and met you."

"As far as I'm concerned all changes have been for the better," he said with a smile, "but there's still one more change you have to make."

"What's that?"

"You're still in exile. Cut yourself loose from your unhappy memories of New York, come home and start afresh. I'd help you get settled."

"I think that's what I'm afraid of." Heavens above, she thought, and cast a shocked glance at the dregs of her whiskey sour. She took a deep breath and tried again. "I mean—"

"You mean you don't want to get involved with me."

"It's not that." She could feel her cheeks burning. "But I just don't want to get hurt. That's all."

She thought he would laugh and make some casual comment to patch the hole which her sharp emotion had torn in the conversation, but he did not laugh. Nor did he make a casual comment. All he said was simply, "If I thought there was a chance of you being hurt I wouldn't have offered to help," and then, taking her hand again so that she was compelled to look at him, he said urgently, "Let me help. Please. I'd like to."

And as he smiled at her and tightened the grip of his hand she knew beyond all doubt that her days in New York were numbered.

2

ONE

There was a strong wind blowing from Ireland, and the shutters of the Rectory-by-the-Sea rattled so hard that they sounded like a host of chattering teeth. The Rectory was an old house with thick whitewashed walls and a well-knit slate roof, but the window frames were not as close fitting as they should have been and Marguerite Stratton had insisted that thick velvet curtains frame each window that faced the sea. Before her second husband had died she had campaigned for the installation of central heating, but Richard Stratton had not felt the cold enough to be discomforted by drafts and had decided that such an expensive innovation must wait until the stock market became less sluggish. Even after Richard had died there had been less money to spare than had been anticipated and Marguerite had again found herself obliged to shelve her heating schemes.

But one day, she thought as she wedged some newspaper into a crack to combat a draft which not even the heavy curtains could quell, one day the house would have central heating. And tomorrow without fail she would persuade Ted to do something about those noisy shutters.

But apart from the shutters and the ill-fitting windows she was well content with the house. It was called the Rectory-by-the-Sea to distinguish it from the Rectory-in-the-Village, a newer house where the present rector now lived. In the old days before the Rectory-in-the-Village had been built and the villages of Cellanporth and Porthmawgan had formed one parish, the rector had lived by the sea in a house which stood halfway between the two villages, but a hundred years ago the bishop of the diocese had assigned each village a clergyman of its own, and after that there was no longer any need for the rector of Cellanporth to be within easy reach of Porthmawgan.

The Rectory-by-the-Sea was windswept and isolated. There was no road along the seashore to connect the two villages for the Downs rose from the beach in a series of humps which would have made building one difficult. A mere farm track linked the house with Cellanporth and only a bridle path curled along the foot of the Downs from the house to Porthmawgan. The roads which did link the two villages were on the other side of the Downs several miles inland.

"A little inaccessible, don't you think?" Marguerite had said tentatively to Richard Stratton after their marriage, but Richard had only said that when he was in the country he enjoyed being inaccessible; besides, since they would be spending part of the year in London there was no need for her to feel condemned to a life of isolation. In fact they had spent little time in London, but Marguerite to her surprise hadn't minded at all. She had found village life far from dull and had become an enthusiastic member of the Women's Institute. After Richard's death people had said to her, "Of course you'll want to move," but Marguerite had discovered that she had no desire to. Although the house, like her income, only had been left to her in trust for life with the reversion going to Guy and Anne, Richard's two children by his first wife, Marguerite felt strongly possessive toward her inheritance. Even without Richard she thought she would be happy enough to stay where she was. They had been married only two years, so it was not as if the house had a lifetime of memories.

Besides, there had been other considerations enticing her to remain at the Rectory. Marguerite, like Richard, had a son by the previous marriage. Ted was twelve years younger than Guy, young enough to live at home during his university vacations but old enough to leave his mother and live elsewhere if he felt so inclined. Ted liked Cellanporth and so long as she stayed there Marguerite felt certain that she would continue to see as much of her son as possible, a prospect which was of paramount importance to her. After all, as she often asked herself, why shouldn't it be? Ted was her only child. Anne was only a stepdaughter and with all her problems was hardly in a position to offer Marguerite much companionship. She had a duty to look after Anne, she realized that, but even so one had to draw the line somewhere. And while she was willing to have Anne living with her she would not—no, simply could not—be entirely responsible for her care.

"She must have a nurse, Guy," she had said firmly to her stepson after the disaster, "or at least a companion who has a nurse's training. . . . Too much to expect of me . . . simply couldn't cope . . . yes, I know it will be a terrible expense, but after all you have an excellent salary, don't you, and Christina had all that money . . ."

And Guy had said, cool as a sea breeze, "We spent it."

"You couldn't have done!" The very idea had seemed blasphemous. Marguerite, who had been brought up in straitened financial circumstances, had a deep and fearful respect for wealth. "You couldn't have spent it all!"

"I handled my salary and I made the mistake of thinking Christina could handle her inheritance. That's all."

"But Guy—"

"You needn't worry," he had said, still very cool. "As you said, I do have a good salary. Anne can have a nurse and you can be let off the hook."

She had disliked him intensely for saying that. After all, it wasn't as if she didn't care about Anne. It wasn't as if she hadn't sincerely wanted to help. But . . . well, there were limits, weren't there? And sometimes one simply had to consider oneself.

She had long since decided it was as well she saw so little of Guy. No wonder Richard had found it difficult to get on with his son! And as for Christina . . .

But there was no point in thinking about Christina.

After stuffing some more newspaper down into another crack she pulled the curtains and crossed the room to turn on an extra bar of the electric fire. The weather had been unseasonably cold lately, more like October than the end of July, but the forecast was good—if one believed in weather forecasts—so perhaps August would bring warmer weather.

The telephone rang.

Ted, she thought at once, Ted's been delayed at the pub, he's met some dreadful tourist, he's phoning to tell me not to wait up for him.

Taking a deep breath she picked up the receiver. "Hullo?"

"Hullo Marguerite, how are you?"

It was Guy. Smothering a sigh of relief she sank down on the edge of the nearest armchair. "Fine, thank you," she said agreeably. "We're all well. Grace took Anne in the car to Castlesea today and I think they both enjoyed themselves. We're all looking forward to seeing you next weekend."

"That's the reason for my call, unfortunately," he said in that casual offhand way of his which she found so irritating. "I'm not going to be able to come down."

"Oh, we *shall* be disappointed! Has something unexpected cropped up?"

"Well, yes," he said. "I suppose you could put it like that. I'm getting married on Saturday."

"Married!" She was so surprised she nearly dropped the receiver. "Are you sure? I mean, did I hear you correctly? You did say 'married,' didn't you?"

"I did and you did." He sounded amused. "I'm sorry I haven't given you more notice, but it's all been very sudden."

"Sudden!" The word struck Marguerite as the grossest understatement she had heard in years. Making an effort to collect her wits she said, "But Guy, dear, who *is* she? Anyone we know?"

"No, her name's Jenny Dexter. She's an English girl Christina and I knew in New York, and she's now living in London."

"How terribly exciting! But why didn't you tell us anything about her before?"

"She hasn't been in London for long."

"But why didn't you give us more notice about the wedding?"

"We only decided to get married a few days ago."

Good heavens, thought Marguerite.

"The wedding's going to be very quiet," Guy was saying. "I've asked Roger Carpenter to be best man, but I really didn't think it was necessary to drag you and Ted up from Cellanporth for the registry office ceremony. Since Jenny and I have both been married before we don't want a big wedding."

"She's divorced?"

"No, a widow. She was married to an American."

"Oh, I see. How old is she?"

"Twenty-one."

"Quite young!" Marguerite almost made some comment about eleven years being a large age gap for a husband and wife to bridge, but fortunately remembered in time that she had been twenty years younger than Guy's father. Instead she said quickly, "Where does she come from?"

"Balham."

"Where?"

"Balham. The London suburb. Surrey."

"Oh . . . she has relatives there, I suppose."

"Yes, her father's a grocer."

"A grocer?"

"Yes."

"Oh, I see," said Marguerite.

There was a slight pause.

"We'll visit you if we may," said Guy, "after we come back from our honeymoon. I'll ring you up as soon as we're in London again."

"Yes, of course—do! We'll all be longing to meet her! Many congratulations, Guy dear, I'm so happy for you."

After two or three more suitable platitudes she replaced the receiver. She allowed herself two full minutes to digest the news and then wasting no more time she dialed the number of the St. Cellan Arms public house where her first husband Leonard Matthews was bartender, proprietor and general factotum.

TWO

"For Christ's sake, love," said Leonard, forgetting that his relationship with his ex-wife was supposed to be "amicable," "can't you leave Ted alone instead of ringing me to check up on him every bloody evening? He's twenty years old and if he hasn't spent a night out on the tiles by now I think it's high time he should. Anyway as it happens he's here helping me clear up in the bar and no scarlet woman has made any effort to seduce him, I regret to say. And now if you don't mind I'm going back to the clearing up."

"Leonard, if you'd just *listen* for a moment instead of leaping to conclusions—"

"There's only one conclusion to leap to whenever you dial my number!"

"Oh, you're impossible! May I speak to Ted at once, please?"

"What for? Leave the boy alone! He'll be home in half an hour! God, when I see the way you carry on sometimes I think it's a bloody miracle he hasn't got a mother complex."

"Leonard, if you don't get Ted this minute—"

"You'll ring off? Go right ahead, love, I'll tell Ted you phoned."

"All right!" shouted Marguerite, suddenly losing her temper. "Tell him his stepbrother's getting married to a grocer's daughter!" And she hung up in high dudgeon.

"Christ!" said Leonard and whistled softly through his teeth.

In the bar Ted had collected the last of the glasses and was preparing to take them out to the kitchen on a large metal tray.

"Guess what," said Leonard, picking up a depleted bottle and deciding to finish the slim measure of whiskey left inside. "That was your mum. Old Guy's getting married again. Didn't wait too long, did he?"

Ted stopped dead. The metal tray in his hands glinted dully in the artificial light.

"Of course I never expected him to stay single more than a year," said Leonard reflectively. "It must get tiring fighting off the beautiful girls. I wonder if she's blonde or brunette. . . . God, some men have all the bloody luck."

Ted set down the tray on top of the bar. "But Guy didn't mention anything about a girl when he was down here last month! When's the wedding going to be?"

"Ask your mum. No good asking me. The only detail she was so gracious as to divulge was that the next Mrs. Guy Stratton is a grocer's daughter, and you can imagine how that set the goose-pimples tingling down your mum's spine."

"Dad," said Ted, "I'd be grateful if you wouldn't speak of my mother in that way. It places me in a very unfair position."

Leonard had the grace to look abashed. "No offense meant, of course," he said quickly, siphoning some soda into his glass of whiskey, "but sometimes your mum's snobbishness gets on my nerves, and I'd be a hypocrite if I said it didn't. As if she had anything to be snobbish about! Marrying a lawyer like Richard Stratton went to her head, if you ask me. Now we're so refined we can't even mention grocers' daughters without a shudder. Good for Guy, is what I say. I'm looking forward to seeing her."

A car door slammed outside. The next moment they heard laughter and the sound of footsteps.

"Did you lock the door of the Private?" said Leonard sharply.

"Oh Lord, I forgot. Sorry, Dad. Shall I—"

"Too late," said Leonard equably as the door of the private bar swung open and a man and a woman, both in their late twenties, strolled across the threshold.

"Hullo Len!" called the man. "How about a couple of whiskey and sodas?"

"And one for you, of course," said the girl sweetly, "and one for Teddy, if he wants to join us."

"No, thank you," said Ted, "and my name's not Teddy, as you well know. You can call me Edward, if you dislike the name Ted so much."

"Heavens, we are a crosspatch tonight!" She slid elegantly onto a bar stool. "How are you, sweetie?" she said casually to Leonard.

"Fine, love," said Leonard. "But we're closed."

"Don't hand us that old line!" protested Charles St. Cellan. "We know as well as you do that your clock's always ten minutes fast!"

"Not tonight it isn't," said Leonard firmly. "Sorry, kids. However, since I can't give you any whiskey I'll give you a choice bit of gossip instead. Who do you think's getting married again just a year after his first wife's tragic and scandalous demise?"

"For God's sake, Dad!" Ted burst out, and then bit his lip and turned away.

"Don't be mean, Teddy darling," said Emma St. Cellan, flicking back a strand of her long hair. "You know Len has to preserve his reputation of knowing everything that goes on in Cellanporth. Don't spoil his fun by being so high minded about gossiping."

"I'm just tired of watching him do anything he can to grab your attention!"

"That's enough, boy," growled Leonard, and Ted, picking up the heavy tray of glasses went out to the kitchen, his mouth turned down at the corners. Then, to the St. Cellans: "Don't mind him—he's in a bit of a mood tonight. Now where was I? Oh yes. Who do you think—"

"Guy Stratton," said Charles, and his sister added with a laugh, "Who's the lucky girl?"

"A grocer's daughter."

"A *what?* Oh Len, don't talk such rubbish!"

"It's true, love. Honest."

"Men like Guy Stratton," said Emma, "contrary to all those lovely fairy tales and Cinderella stories, do *not*, repeat *not,* marry grocers' daughters. They marry heiresses. Rich beautiful girls with nice fat bank balances—"

"Emmy dear," said her brother, "you really do sound very bitchy. I'd watch that if I were you."

"Oh shut up!"

They smiled at one another affectionately.

"Well, I think you're wrong this time, love," said Leonard, "no matter what you say. This little girl probably doesn't have a penny to her name."

"I'll bet you three dry martinis that she does," said Emma St. Cellan. "Grocer's daughter or no grocer's daughter." And she added lightly with a wry smile, "I think I know Guy better than you do."

THREE

Later that night as they drove back to Trecellan Hall after wheedling two rounds of drinks from Leonard, Charles said to his sister, "I wonder how much Guy's told his fiancee about Christina."

"Everything, I expect," said Emma. "Keeping deadly secrets about the first wife is all rather old hat now, don't you think? Why? Thinking of a spot of blackmail?"

"What a vulgar idea!"

"It might help pay some of your bills since you refuse to take a job!"

"I'm a partner in our boutique in Castlesea, aren't I? Anyway I've paid all the important bills for the time being so I can't see why it's necessary for me to stoop to a life of crime to support us both!"

"You might at least do me the favor of marrying an heiress. If Guy Stratton can keep doing it, why can't you?

You're just as tall, dark and handsome as he is—and more blue-blooded too, if one's fussy about that kind of thing. Of course, you're stupider than Guy, but an heiress in love isn't necessarily going to notice that."

"Practice what you preach, dear girl," said Charles with a yawn. "Incidentally, are you sure Guy will have told his fiancee everything? I mean, do you suppose he's told her about us?"

"What an awful egoist you are, Charles. Why on earth should he?"

"Well, after all, it was our party—"

"I don't want to think about that," said Emma.

"And let's face it, darling, it was quite a party. You know, sometimes I wish I could remember it more clearly."

"The less either of us remember, the better. We were damned lucky not to end up in jail."

"Someone was damned lucky not to end up on trial at the Old Bailey."

"Drop it, Charles, would you? I don't want to think about that any more—and neither I'm sure does Guy."

"I wouldn't blame him if he hasn't told his little grocer's daughter everything. After all," said Charles St. Cellan meditatively, "there's no denying that sometimes there are things it's better not to know."

FOUR

"Letter from London for you, Dr. Carpenter," said Mrs. Williams, bringing the post to the table where Roger was eating his usual solitary breakfast. She spoke of London as if it were an amalgamation of Sodom and Gomorrah, and handed him the envelope with fingers that she wiped afterwards on her apron. "Bad news, I shouldn't wonder."

"Why bad?" said Roger vaguely. He had been out most
of the night; a baby had decided to enter the world early.
As he took the letter he was wondering whether he could
snatch an hour's sleep after his surgery closed at nine-
thirty and before it was time for him to leave for the
Porthmawgan Cottage Hospital where he was a consul-
tant.

"No good ever came out of cities," said Mrs. Williams.
"Cities are places where men gather to defy the Lord."

"Um," said Roger, recognizing Guy Stratton's hand-
writing on the envelope. "Is there any more tea?" As she
left the room he broke the seal and took out the folded
slip of notepaper.

My dear Roger,

*I know how very busy you are, but I'm writing to ask if
you could do me a large favor. I've decided to get married
again and I'm in desperate need of a best man. Is there
any chance of you snatching some time off next Saturday
to give me moral support at Caxton Hall? I realize that
this is a long way for you to come for such a brief ceremony, but there's no one I'd rather have.*

*A word of warning: I haven't invited Marguerite or
Ted to the wedding, although I know I should have, so
you'll have to tread carefully in that direction. I'm going
to phone Marguerite with the news and hope to convince
her that I'm doing her a favor by not inviting her; with
luck I'll be able to avoid offending her. As for Ted, he'll
be only too glad to escape—he hates both weddings and
London. That leaves Anne, and of course there's no
question of her being present. But could you try and ex-*

plain to her what's happening? You're the only one she ever seems to understand.

I hope to see you soon and hear from you sooner.

> *Yours,*
> *Guy*

P.S. Jenny is small, very pretty and a redhead. You'll like her.

Mrs. Williams returned with a fresh pot of tea. "Bad news, doctor?"

"No, on the contrary. Guy Stratton's getting married again."

"And his first wife barely one year in her grave," said Mrs. Williams sonorously.

"It sounds as if his fiancee is very nice," said Roger, thinking absently how accustomed he had become to ignoring ninety percent of his housekeeper's conversation. "I hope he'll be happy. He certainly deserves to be after all the trouble he's had."

"Wickedness begets tragedy," said Mrs. Williams. "Will you be in for lunch today, doctor?"

He told her he would eat at the hospital, gulped down a third cup of tea and hurried to his surgery in the south wing of the house. Five patients were already in the waiting room to see him, and soon he was engrossed in their troubles, but even as he listened he knew there would be no chance of a nap before he went to the hospital. Instead he would have to take his car and drive all the way down that bumpy cart track which led from the village to the Rectory-by-the-Sea.

FIVE

"I'm so glad to see you, Roger," said Marguerite, coming out to meet him as he left his car and crossed the yard to the back door. "I did phone your surgery but you'd just left. Isn't it wonderful news about Guy? Since you're to be best man I presume he's given you more advance notice than we've had of the wedding."

"It's splendid news, isn't it? When did Guy tell you?"

"He phoned last night. Anne and Grace were both in bed by that time, but I told Grace this morning and she said we should consult you before we told Anne."

"That was sensible of her. Are they upstairs in Anne's sitting room?"

They were. The room overlooked the sea, and Anne would sit on the window seat for hours watching the gulls swoop over the vast expanse of sand. She was there now as he entered the room; the light slanted across her fair hair and shone on the clear angles of her face so that he thought as he had so often before how beautiful she was.

"Hullo Anne," he said.

She glanced at him fleetingly before turning back to the sea.

He nodded at her companion. "Hullo Grace."

"Good morning, Roger." Grace Reid had been a nurse at the Porthmawgan Cottage Hospital and Roger had recommended her when Guy had been looking for someone to care for his sister. She was a good companion, strong and capable, and she also had the virtue of not being too talkative. What she did say was always briskly pertinent, and Roger, admiring this quality which kept their relationship on an impersonal basis, no longer worried about her underlying intensity, the passion which aroused all his bachelor's defensive instincts.

He said carefully to her in a low voice, "Marguerite told you the news, I hear."

"Yes." She stood up. "I'll leave you with Anne for a moment."

"Thanks." He waited till she had gone before he sat down beside Anne on the window seat. Outside the sun was obscured by a passing cloud and a shadow had spread far out over the beach to the cliffs and beyond the cliffs to the black arm of the bay known as the Snake's Tail.

"Anne, we've heard some news about Guy."

The tide was coming in and the waves were licking greedily over the dry sand.

"Guy wrote and said he's fallen in love again."

There was a bank of cloud on the horizon. Maybe it would rain later.

"The girl's called Jenny—and she's only a little older than you, Anne. He's going to marry her soon and bring her down here so that you can meet her."

Anne's eyes were green. He remembered how he had always thought her eyes were blue; it was only after he had begun to see her professionally that he had realized they weren't blue at all.

"Anne, you're going to have a new sister-in-law. What do you think of that?"

The girl turned her head slowly as if her neck were stiff and gave him a small secret smile. "I think I'm going to kill her," she said.

3

Jenny invited her father and stepmother to the wedding but was secretly relieved when her stepmother claimed to have "a touch of flu" and backed out. Since her return to England two months earlier, Jenny had visited her family only twice and neither visit had been an unqualified success.

"Well, it's nice to know you came to your senses at last," her father said during the first visit. "I'm sure I don't know why you thought this country wasn't good enough for you."

"Now Dad, it wasn't that—"

"Well, we're not surprised you came back, are we, Jack?" said her stepmother. "Judging from all one sees on the telly America's no fit place to live nowadays."

Jenny found it very difficult not to lose her temper.

Later, when she rented a flat in Kensington she invited them to see her new home, but only her father came. His arrival coincided with one of Guy's visits and there was a moment of awkwardness as she introduced them. But after Guy had gone her father said, "Well, you certainly

36

know how to pick them, don't you?" And beneath his glum tone she detected a ring of pride. "Who is he anyway?"

"An architect I met in New York."

"Is he your latest?"

"We do see quite a bit of one another, if that's what you mean."

"He's married, I suppose," said her father.

"A widower," said Jenny coldly.

"Well, that's something, I must say. What with all that goes on nowadays a father hardly knows what to expect from his daughter. Now, you be careful and sensible and don't make a fool of yourself—"

"Dad," she said with a smile, "you don't have to worry about me. You really don't."

"Of course I have to worry about you! A young girl like you all alone in a big city—well, it's just not right somehow. . . . You'd better make sure some man doesn't try to marry you for all that American money you've got. I mean, anything could happen, couldn't it, if you weren't level-headed and sensible."

"I'll be sensible," she promised him, but later when she told him she was going to marry Guy he said at once, "Is he well off?"

"Dad, he has a marvelous salary!"

"Well, all the same . . . why don't you wait a month or two? Don't go losing your head and doing something you'll live to regret."

"But I don't want to wait! I'm sure of my own feelings, and besides it isn't as if I'd just met Guy—I knew him for some time in New York."

But she did not tell her father that Guy—the new Guy

she loved so much—was a different man from the Guy she had known in New York. Nor did she disclose any details of his first wife's death.

Guy did not like to talk about it. Late one night she summoned enough courage to ask him what had happened at the party, but he merely said, "No one knew for certain. It was confused when everyone moved from the house to the sea—some people stayed up on the cliffs, others took the path to the beach, a lot of people lost sight of one another, and everyone, including Christina, was stoned."

"You mean there were no witnesses to her death?" said Jenny incredulously.

"None."

"But who found her dead?"

"I did. The next morning on the beach. Her body was twisted and sodden and there was wet sand everywhere, even on her eyeballs, because the tide . . ." He stopped. When he could speak again he said rapidly, "I'm sorry, I just don't want to talk about it. I hope you understand, but—"

"Of course I understand!" she exclaimed upset, and after that she avoided mentioning either the party or Christina. Her eagerness to avoid the past even made her reluctant to question Guy about his sister, but although she continually expected Guy to tell her more about Anne, he seemed to take great care to avoid referring to her. After a while this omission made Jenny feel uneasy, but she told herself she was foolish to worry. If there was any great mystery about Anne, Guy would already have told her about it. Besides, the details of Anne's nervous breakdown were none of her business.

In an effort to turn her mind from the past she tried to concentrate on her new flat, her readjustment to English life, and later the introduction which Guy provided to the London theaters and restaurants.

"But you can't be such a stranger to the West End," protested Guy, amused by her unexpected ignorance of the pleasures he took for granted. "Anyone would think you came from John o' Groats instead of a London suburb!"

"Balham seemed just as far away," she said, trying not to sound too defensive. She knew Guy was not a snob and could not have cared less about her background, but he seemed to have no understanding of the problems that her background might have created. It was easy to profess class prejudice to be obsolete and even easier to declare oneself classless if one had been born in the right place, educated at the right schools and offered the right place in the right profession. "We hardly ever went up to the West End," she explained to Guy. "We'd usually wait until the sales were on and then we'd come up on the tube and have lunch at Lyons." She might have been describing life on another planet.

"How on earth did you adjust to life as a millionaire's wife?" was all he said in amazement when she had finished, and she had to remind him that Harlan had avoided living like a millionaire and flaunting his rich relatives. "I did have to make some adjustments, of course," she added honestly, "but I was still so busy adjusting to America that I didn't notice them at the time. Being in a foreign country had an odd effect on me. Everything that had mattered in England—class and so on—didn't seem to matter in America. It was as if I'd shed my identity and found a new one. Perhaps that was why I was reluctant to come back to England—I thought I might have to go back to being my old self."

"Only you don't, of course. Darling, you're not trying to tell me you're still hung up on this absurd class nonsense?"

It was useless trying to explain further. She decided to shrug off the subject as best as she could. "I'm hung up on my identity," she said with a smile. "I'm no longer the old Jenny and yet now I'm not the American Jenny either. I feel very confused sometimes."

But Guy helped unravel her confusion. She had long known she felt physically attracted to him; soon she knew the attraction went deeper than a mere appreciation of his looks. She liked his confidence; amidst all her worries about resettling in London she found his assurance endlessly soothing. There was no need to worry if Guy was at hand, and she liked the concern for her that she knew was genuine, his willingness to help, his generosity, the many ways, some obvious, some subtle, in which he let her know he cared.

From the beginning she had been prepared for the inevitable proposition and was almost annoyed when he persisted in maintaining a low-keyed relationship with her, but after a while she realized that Guy had his reasons for his cautious behavior. He had already made one disastrous attempt to seduce her; this time, she realized, he was determined to make no move until he was certain of success. Yet when the move did come it was in a form which caught her unprepared.

"You know, I spend so much time at your flat I think it would easier if I moved in," he said casually as he accepted the cup of coffee she passed him across the dining room table one evening. "Are you doing anything next Saturday? Maybe we could get married."

Her hand nearly knocked over the milk jug. She heard herself say in an astonished voice, "Married? Me?" And then, stupidly, "You?"

"Well, I dare say marriage does sound old-fashioned to a young thing like you, but when one's over thirty it's amazing how attractive these old institutions suddenly seem." He was teasing her but his eyes were serious and she was aware of his extreme stillness as he waited for her reaction.

"Oh, but . . ." She was so overcome that she could no longer speak. Joy, elation and shock rushed through her mind in a jumbled whirl until finally all she could manage to say was, "Could we really be married as soon as next Saturday? I'm sure there must be some law saying we can't!"

"I'll find out," said Guy, and did. The proposed wedding date did in fact have to be postponed for a few days until all the bureaucratic regulations were satisfied, but within a month she was standing with Guy in one of the quiet rooms at Caxton Hall and listening to the brief informal words of the civil wedding ceremony.

"I hope you'll be happy," said her father afterwards. "I still think you should have waited longer, but it's done now so there's no use crying over spilled milk. Just remember there's always your bedroom waiting for you at home if there's any trouble."

"Oh *Dad!*" Jenny hissed at him, and stole an anxious glance at her husband, but Guy was busy talking to his best man.

"I don't object to him, mind," said her father. "He seems all right to me, but you haven't known him long and—"

"Dad, will you stop! Please!"

"All right, all right! No need to get narked just because I express some natural concern for my only child! Well, I don't suppose either of you'll want to come and see us very often, but—"

"We'll visit you after the honeymoon," said Jenny firmly. "I'll phone you." To her relief they were interrupted at that point by Guy, and presently Jenny's father stumped off to minister to his wife's purported case of influenza.

"Your father doesn't like me much," Guy observed ruefully later. "I'm sorry he wouldn't join us here for lunch."

"Here" was the Hotel Dorchester.

"Oh, that's just his manner," said Jenny hastily. "He always pretends not to like anything or anyone."

"I feel sorry for him missing some first-class champagne," said Guy's best man Roger Carpenter cheerfully, and raised his glass to his lips in appreciation.

She had decided she liked Dr. Carpenter. He was an energetic man of thirty-five with receding fair hair, innocent blue eyes and a good-natured mouth. He had a habit of listening to a conversation with his head tilted slightly to one side and an expression of intense concentration on his face, two mannerisms cultivated, she suspected, by the desire to appear totally absorbed in his patients' troubles. The mannerisms were disconcerting; Jenny found herself beginning to wonder whether he was as attentive as he appeared to be.

"Well, Guy," he was saying as he set down his glass, "when can we expect to see you and Jenny in Cellan-porth?"

"In about a month, I should think. We'll be away for a week, and when we get back I'll have to spend some days at the office before I can take more time off. . . ."

But Roger wasn't listening. Jenny was sure he wasn't even though he still had his head tilted and appeared to be concentrating. To confirm her suspicions he interrupted unexpectedly, "Will you be staying at the Rectory as usual?"

"Where else should we stay! Yes, of course. Why?"

"No special reason. I'm just a little concerned about Anne, that's all. She seemed to be muddling Jenny with Christina."

There was a small pause.

"But surely—" Guy began, and stopped.

"I think it's only a transitory confusion," said Roger quickly. "She simply needs more time to adjust to the idea that you have a wife again—and that the wife isn't Christina."

Guy said nothing.

Roger looked at him sharply before turning to Jenny. "Guy's told you about Anne's problems, of course."

"Yes," Jenny heard herself say. "Yes, he told me she'd had a nervous breakdown." But as soon as she spoke she knew that Guy had not been honest with her and that Anne's troubles went deeper than he had led her to suppose.

There was a longer, heavier silence. At last Roger said evenly to Guy, "Phone me before you arrange your visit and I'll be able to give you an up-to-date report on how she is."

"All right. Yes, of course." As if making a sudden decision he glanced directly at Jenny across the table. "Anne did have a nervous breakdown," he said in a rapid voice. "Or at least that's how I, as a layman, would describe it. How would one describe Anne's illness in professional terms, Roger? A psychotic episode? I remember something was said about schizophrenia—"

"There were manifestations of schizophrenia," said Roger, not looking at either of them. He was toying uncomfortably with his fork. "But there's been an improvement since then."

After a moment Jenny said. "Since when?"

"Since the incident," said Roger embarrassed. "There was a party—a wild party given by a thoroughly unpleasant local couple—"

"It was the night Christina died," Guy said, and suddenly the color was gone from his face and the lines of strain were deep about his mouth. "Someone slipped Anne a dose of LSD."

TWO

What jolted Jenny even more than the discovery of the source of Anne's illness was the fact that Guy had withheld the knowledge from her. She found it impossible to believe his silence had sprung from a desire to protect her; she knew well enough what went on in the world—and what had gone on at one or two of the wilder parties the Strattons had given in Manhattan. So why had Guy found it so hard to talk to her about Anne? Perhaps he had thought the knowledge would have prejudiced her against his sister, but surely he knew that although Jenny possessed certain firm notions about the way she herself should behave, she was not a person who made rigid moral judgments on others. She could only conclude that either Guy did not know her or that he did not trust her, and although she tried to hide her feelings in front of Roger, she felt both puzzled and hurt.

Guy sensed her feelings. He had no chance to discuss the matter with her immediately, for after Roger left they had to rush to the airport, but later, once their luggage had sailed away on the appropriate conveyor belt, he suggested they have a drink before their flight was called. No sooner had they sat down that he said, "I'm sorry I didn't give you a full explanation about Anne before, but the fact is I feel so damned guilty where she's concerned that it's very difficult for me to bring myself to talk about it."

"But Guy—"

"I did mean to tell you she was at that party," he said troubled. "Of course I meant to tell you, but I kept putting it off and putting it off—"

"But why should you have felt guilty?" said Jenny, trying to sound calm. An answer to her question flashed through her mind before she had finished speaking but it was so distasteful that she could not put in into words.

"Because afterwards it seemed as bad as if I'd given Anne the LSD myself. I didn't, of course—" He was so intent on recalling the past that he fortunately failed to notice Jenny's expression of relief "—but the incident still places me in an appallingly bad light. Which was no doubt the main reason why I shied away from telling you the whole story."

He picked up his glass to take another sip but put it down again untasted. "You see, I took Anne to the party—well, that was reasonable enough because she'd been feeling low since my father died and I thought the evening out would cheer her up. I also hoped she might

meet someone interesting there because she'd been away
at boarding school so she didn't know many people in the
neighborhood. So Christina and I took her with us. And
that was all we—I—did. Took her with us and forgot
about her. Even when I saw what kind of a party it was
turning into I didn't bother about Anne. I was too absorbed in myself and . . . other people. It wasn't until the
next morning that I heard that Anne had disappeared.
She was eventually found soaked to the skin in one of the
caves below the cliffs—she refused to let anyone come
near her at first, but finally Roger and the ambulance men
managed to—" He stopped.

Jenny was appalled. "You mean she's never really been
herself since then?"

"That was the god-awful part. We kept waiting and
waiting for her to get back to normal, and she never did.
In fact for a time she got worse—she spent a month in a
nursing home and several specialists saw her. Finally she
did get a little better and that was when I engaged Grace
Reid to look after her full-time and brought her back to
the Rectory. Roger is convinced that she'll eventually
make a full recovery and sometimes she does seem to be
almost herself again, but then she still has days when she
won't speak or days when she speaks but makes no sense.
I often wonder if she'll ever return to normal."

"What a dreadful thing to happen." Jenny shuddered.
She found now that she could understand Guy's reluc-
tance to discuss the tragedy, and since the mystery had
been explained it was easier for her to sympathize with
him. "Poor Anne. And poor you."

"Me! I was responsible for the whole damned disaster!"

"In a way, perhaps, but . . . well, Anne was eighteen,

wasn't she? I know it was an off-key party and you probably should have taken her home, but at eighteen one should be able to look after oneself. I don't think you should blame yourself entirely."

"But Anne had always lived a protected life—she was young for her age. I think it was connected with the fact that she was an afterthought, born when my father was over fifty. He was more like a doting grandfather than a sensible parent where Anne was concerned. She was always treated as if she were a little girl, someone who had to be cosseted and given special care, and it never occurred to me to question this until I discussed it with Roger after her breakdown. He thought it probable that Anne's emotional development had been arrested and that she might have had mental problems later anyway. Apparently people who are unhinged by an LSD experience very often have some deep-seated emotional problem which they may or may not have been aware of beforehand."

There was a pause before Jenny said, "No wonder you changed after that party!"

"Yes, after a night which had such dreadful repercussions it's hardly surprising that I should have felt such revulsion toward the kind of life I'd been living." He slipped his arm around her and drew her closer to him. "But let's not talk of that any more. All we need think about at the moment is our flight to Venice and how hot the weather will be and what kind of a view we'll have from our hotel suite. . . ."

Jenny certainly had no wish to think of anything else. Her curiosity about Anne had been more than satisfied, and her bewilderment about Guy's silence had been smoothed away by his frank explanation. Closing her mind to all thought of the disastrous party she turned with relief to the honeymoon awaiting them in Venice.

The hotel was very grand and very sumptuous and, to Jenny's Americanized eyes, very European. Gilt decoration, baroque furnishings and acres of plump red carpet produced an illusion of another age; cocooned in such an old-world atmosphere, Jenny settled down to savor the breakfasts on their private balcony which overlooked the Lido, the idleness of mornings on the beach, the languid explorations of the long afternoons, the formal dinners in a dining room where musicians still played Strauss waltzes, and later, much later, the glint of moonlight on dark waters and the fresh whiteness of the linen on their enormous double bed.

Harlan began for the first time to seem remote to her.

"Like a fairy tale," she said to Guy. "The one where the beggar-maid married the prince and lived happily ever after."

"Except that in real life she didn't."

"Harlan used to blame me for that." Pangs of insecurity edged back to haunt her. "Oh Guy, it's all right, isn't it? With us, I mean. You're not simply pretending it's all right just to be nice to me?"

"Darling, what extraordinary things you say sometimes!"

"But Harlan used to say—"

"It's plain to see that Harlan made you take the blame for something that was probably his fault. There's no other reason why you should have such a poor opinion of yourself."

"Well, I know you must think I'm so ignorant and inexperienced about so many things—"

"I'm tired of women who know everything," said Guy. "I didn't marry you in the hope that you'd turn out to be one of those tiresome sex manuals. And just in case you're getting a Christina complex—"

"Oh no!" said Jenny too quickly.

"I thought you were!"

"Well, I did admire Christina very much at one time. She was so glamorous and sophisticated—"

"Oh yes," said Guy, "that was a great comfort to me when she started seeking a cure for her frigidity by sleeping around with other men."

"You mean—"

"Darling, you can forget poor Christina. Feel sorry for her if you must, but don't ever fall into the trap of envying her because I can promise you that there was nothing for you to envy."

Jenny did indeed feel better after that. She was grateful to Guy for understanding her fears about Christina, and his understanding gave her the confidence she needed. Her only regret arose at the end of their visit when they had to exchange the luxury of their hotel for the more prosaic surroundings of the flat in Kensington, but she soon discovered she had no time to sigh nostalgically for Venice. Guy's friends, new friends he had made since Christina's death, asked them to dinner; the ritual visit to her parents had to be made; new friends of her own suggested shopping expeditions and lunches. Before Jenny was aware of it a month had passed since their return from Italy and Guy was beginning to talk about the extra week's holiday he planned to take in mid-September.

"I know it'll probably be boring for you," he said apologetically, "but I think you'll like the scenery at Cellan-

porth, if nothing else. The sea will seem like the Arctic
Ocean after the Mediterranean, but maybe if we feel particularly brave we might paddle."

"I don't see why I should be bored—don't be so
gloomy!" She felt a tremor of dread at the thought of
meeting Anne, so to divert herself she said quickly, "Tell
me more about your stepmother and stepbrother—you've
said so little about them."

They had just finished their Sunday breakfast and were
lingering at the table as they drank the last of the coffee.
The flat that she had taken on returning to London was
spacious and comfortable; Jenny thought again how glad
she was that Guy had suggested they should continue to
live there after their marriage, for it would have been tedious for her to have begun yet another search for a new
home. Guy had previously been living off the Edgeware
Road in a cramped service flatlet which had surprised
Jenny by its dinginess, and she had wondered if he were
reacting against the expensive apartments he had provided for Christina. She doubted if he had been motivated by
a desire to economize, for when at last they steeled themselves to discuss their finances he at once declared, "We'll
live on my salary, of course."

Jenny realized that his pride was involved. She tried to
be tactful. "All right," she said. "We'll live on your salary
and supplement it with my income whenever we like."
And before he could comment she rushed on: "I'd like to
think of Harlan's money as if it were an old-fashioned
dowry—I wish you'd manage it for me, Guy. I still feel
guilty about inheriting so much from Harlan and I'd
much rather have as little to do with it as possible."

"Well, we could have a joint account, I suppose—"

"Oh yes," said Jenny thankfully, "a joint account. And

you pay all the bills. I've always thought anyway that husbands should be in charge of the family finances."

"Very unliberated!" laughed Guy, but the awkwardness had been glossed over and the subject was settled. They never discussed money again. Jenny privately congratulated herself on the way she had handled the situation, and settled down to spend their money without undue extravagance. She did buy some more new furniture for the flat, but that, as she told herself, was money well spent, and now as she and Guy lingered in the dining alcove she decided the flat was the most pleasing home she had ever had. She sighed contentedly. On the sofa in the other half of the L-shaped living room the Sunday newspapers were waiting for them and beyond the window the sky had the pale clarity of parchment. A transistor radio drooled on top of the china cabinet; Guy reached to switch off the music just as an announcer intervened to promise cool winds, brief showers and the imminent arrival of a trough of low pressure from the Atlantic.

"I hope the weather improves by the time we arrive at Cellanporth," said Guy ruefully. "My father's house is just above the beach and stands foursquare to every breath of bad weather from the sea." And he told her how his father, who had long cherished the idea of retiring to the country, had quickly become disillusioned during the two years he had spent at the Rectory.

"He was soon bored with Cellanporth," Guy added, "although he would never admit it either to himself or to anyone else. If it hadn't been for Marguerite I believe he would have moved back to London, but he was happy with her and the happiness took the edge off his disappointment."

"Had he known her long before he married her?"

"Yes, strangely enough he was her first husband's solicitor and acted for Leonard at the time of the divorce. That was—let me see, how long ago was it? Fifteen years at least because Ted was only a very small boy at the time. But when my father first met Marguerite he was happily married to my mother. He did take a liking to Leonard, though, whose run of bad luck at that time included bankruptcy as well as divorce, and it was through my father that Leonard became proprietor of the St. Cellan Arms. My father had been born and brought up in Castlesea, the nearest large town to Cellanporth, and he knew the St. Cellans, who owned most of Cellanporth including the pub. It so happened at the time that the old squire— who's now dead—was looking for a new landlord and was willing to consider Leonard when my father recommended him for the job. Fortunately it turned out well. Leonard's too unconventional to last long in a nine-to-five job but he's sociable and no fool and he soon made a name for himself at the pub."

"But wasn't it awkward when your father married Marguerite later and brought her to live at the Rectory?"

"Not really, because that was much later, at least twelve years after the divorce, and by that time Leonard and Marguerite were supposed to be on friendly terms. I say 'supposed to be' because my father actually met Marguerite again during one of their squabbles. They had reached an impasse on the subject of how much Leonard was to contribute to Ted's education, and Leonard had asked my father to negotiate with Marguerite. My father had by that time spent three very miserable years being a widower and was more than ready for remarriage. Before we knew what was happening he himself was volunteering to pay Ted's school bills."

"Were you pleased?"

"When my father remarried? I suppose so, although I wasn't particularly enamored with the prospect of having Marguerite for a stepmother. But she did make my father happy and I've always tried to be as pleasant to her as possible."

"Why don't you like her?"

"Oh . . ." Guy sighed. "Dislike is too strong a word. Antipathy would be better. I just find her tiresome." He was smiling at her. Beyond the window the white skies had darkened and rain was falling lightly on the dripping leaves of the square. "Do you still want to go to Cellanporth?"

"Of course! Don't be silly!" She stood up, moved over to him impulsively and kissed him on the lips. When her mouth was free she repeated, to convince herself as much as to convince him, "I really am looking forward to meeting your family, Guy—no matter what you say about them!" But even though she did her best to sound lighthearted she had to admit privately to herself that the visit to Cellanporth seemed certain to be an ordeal.

THREE

Ted was feeling mutinous, in one of his moods when he felt like hitchhiking to the Himalayas and embarking on a prolonged study of Zen. Other people did it so why shouldn't he? But there was no answer to that except that he hated conforming to anything, even popular trends, and besides he had reasons for wanting to stay at Cellan-porth.

His mutinous mood had begun when his mother had asked him to drive her Ford Cortina to the station at Castlesea to meet Guy and Jenny. The request itself was harmless enough; he liked to drive the Cortina and was as curious as anyone in Cellanporth to see his stepbrother's new wife. But Marguerite had asked him to put on a suit and tie.

"Why?" he demanded.

"Well, dear, it *is* rather a special occasion."

"What's wrong with a sports shirt?"

"Nothing, dear. On the right occasions."

"At least I keep my hair cut. Isn't that enough sacrifice for me to make in the name of respectability?"

"Heavens," said Marguerite, trying not to sound an-noyed, "you sound just like your father."

Ted turned aside to hide his pleasure and with an ap-pearance of sulkiness trudged upstairs to change.

The door to Anne's sitting room was ajar. Roger Carpenter was in the sitting room talking to her, and Ted found himself pausing to listen to their conversation.

Anne was saying in an anxious but quiet voice, "Sup-posing she doesn't like me?"

"Of course she'll like you, Anne."

There was a silence. Ted was just straining his ears to catch Anne's reply when a low voice said behind him, "You do like to eavesdrop, don't you?" and swinging around he found himself face to face with Grace Reid.

To his fury he felt himself blush. Grace, with her brisk authority, reminded him of the school mistress who had supervised his sessions at kindergarten sixteen years ago.

Beyond them in the room Anne was saying defiantly, "I shan't like her. I know I shan't."

"But Anne my dear—"

Ted pushed past Grace and blundered into the room. "Anne, do you want to come with me into Castlesea to meet Guy?"

"Ted!" said Grace sharply, but he took no notice.

Roger swung around. "That's a good idea, Ted," he said steadily, "but I think Anne wants to stay here this morning."

"Anne has a lot to do," Grace said crisply. "I've promised to set her hair for her, and when it's dry she has to change into her new dress. By the way, Anne, why don't you wear the brooch Guy brought you from New York? It's so pretty and Guy would be pleased to see you wearing it."

"Oh yes," said Anne vaguely, and wandered over to the chest of drawers in search of her jewel box.

"I must be on my way," said Roger abruptly. "I'll call in later on, Grace, to see how things are going."

Ted walked out of the room but Roger joined him on the landing before he could complete his escape.

"Ted. Just a moment, please."

Ted stopped, feeling angry again, and shoved his fists into his pockets. Roger closed the door of Anne's room quietly before turning to face him.

"That was a silly thing to do, don't you think?"

"I don't see why."

"You know perfectly well that Grace and I have been working hard to make this confrontation easy and natural for Anne, a meeting which can take place in her own surroundings where she runs the least possible risk of being unduly disturbed. Why disrupt all our plans by putting the idea of a trip to Castlesea into her head? I can think of nothing more likely to disturb her."

"I think you disturb Anne more than I do! She's always happy when she's with me—it's only when you come that she gets nervous and upset!"

"If that were true I'd ask another doctor to attend Anne," said Roger, who hated scenes but was finding it difficult to keep his temper. "But since it isn't true—"

"Ted!" called Marguerite from downstairs. "You're going to be late! Oughtn't you to be on your way?"

"All right!" yelled Ted, and going into his bedroom, slammed the door.

It was an hour's drive to Castlesea and the wet roads and leaden skies suited his mood. However, after he had parked the car he noticed that the clouds had parted in the west and the glimpse of blue sky raised his spirits so that he forgot to brood on Roger Carpenter and began instead to search for some sign of the London train. Despite Marguerite's fears he was early; he had to wait ten minutes before the train drew up at the platform, and during that time the last of the rain swept away to the east and the sun began to shine strongly on that grimy industrial port and sparkle upon the shifting waters of the harbor.

Guy stepped from the train and turned to offer his hand to the girl following him.

She was pretty. She had a small straight nose, a shy smile and wide dark eyes. Her hair, which was a deep shade of red, was piled up onto the top of her head and fastened there in a precarious bunch of curls. The style made her look older than she was, but as Ted drew nearer he decided that the freckles on the bridge of her nose offset this hopeful attempt to appear sophisticated.

He smiled at her politely and tried not to think of Christina.

"Jenny," said Guy to his wife, "this is Ted."

Jenny saw a tall young man with narrow blue eyes and a stubborn mouth. He wore a gray suit which could have fitted him better, a white shirt which had failed to drip-dry without wrinkles as it should have done, and a pale mauve knitted tie. His smile was gentle, at odds with the air of sullenness which clung to him.

"Hullo," he said awkwardly and offered her a large bony hand.

"Hi," said Jenny equally awkward, and slipped her hand into his to be shaken.

"How's everything?" asked Guy.

"Okay. Can I help you with those suitcases?"

Some confused minutes followed while the two men rescued the luggage, but at last the boot of the Cortina was closed over the last suitcase and Guy was sliding into the back seat beside Jenny while Ted sat alone in the front.

Just like a ruddy chauffeur, thought Ted.

He glanced at his stepbrother in the mirror as the car edged out of the car park, and Guy, intercepting the glance, said pleasantly, "This is good of you, Ted. I'm sorry to have had to drag you all the way into Castlesea like this, but since my car's out of action I thought it best to come down by train."

One of Guy's cleverest assets, Ted decided, was his trick of knowing when to say the right thing. "That's okay," he said laconically. "What happened to your car?"

"Some fool ran into it when it was parked outside our flat . . ." Guy embarked on a description of the accident, and the miles slipped past as the Cortina headed west.

It was early evening by the time they reached Cellanporth. The urban sprawl of Castlesea had faded into wooded countryside, but finally all trees were left behind as the car headed toward a ridge of low bare hills on the horizon. The fields were now bordered not by fences but by stone walls; ambling cows had been replaced by motionless sheep; the farms were further apart, the villages were more scattered. The mark of the twentieth century blurred into those sweeping views over the open landscape. The Cortina seemed enormous in the narrow lanes, and although Ted drove carefully Jenny found her foot pressing hard against an imaginary brake each time the car approached a blind corner.

"Nearly there," said Guy.

The hills were closer now; Jenny saw that the road wound through a narrow pass before falling into unknown territory beyond, and presently Ted changed gear as the car began to climb. Minutes later the Cortina had puffed to the crest of the ridge and there before them lay the sea.

Jenny gasped. Guy had mentioned the remoteness of St. Cellan's Bay and had implied that Cellanporth stood amidst attractive scenery, but nothing he had said had conveyed the splendor of the bare grassy hills sloping to the miles of white beach far below or the magnificence of the tall cliffs on the southern headland of the bay. The headland narrowed into a long undulating arm which jutted out to sea, and although distance made it difficult to be certain, Jenny thought that the end of the arm was an island.

"That's the Snake's Tail," said Guy. "It's cut off from

the mainland at high tide, but at low tide you can walk out to the very tip of the peninsula."

"But it's all beautiful!" Jenny was still marveling at the view. "Do many people come out here?"

"On summer weekends unfortunately yes, but we're at the end of the holiday season now so there shouldn't be too many coaches descending on us. Luckily the average day tripper hates to walk and so as it's a ten-minute scramble down to the beach from the village most of the visitors merely potter about on top of the cliffs—or at most wander out along the headland to the coastguard station where they can have a good view across the causeway to the Snake's Tail. The beach below Cellanporth is never crowded, although Porthmawgan is a different story because the beach is more accessible there."

"Where's Porthmawgan?"

"Right at the other end of the bay—can you see the dunes in the distance? Beyond the dunes there's an estuary, and a small harbor. Ted's father keeps his boat there."

"Guy, that white house all on its own at the bottom of the hills . . ."

"Yes, that's the Rectory-by-the-Sea."

"What a wonderful position!"

"You wouldn't think it so wonderful if you had to live there in winter. It gets very damp and cold, doesn't it, Ted?"

"You get used to it," said Ted. He disliked the deprecating note in Guy's voice. To change the subject he said abruptly to Jenny, "These are the outskirts of Cellanporth—as you can see, it's not a large village. My father's pub is at the other end, out toward the headland. You'll be able to see it just before we turn off past the church."

The church, ancient, weathered and squat, rose above

a tousled graveyard to peer out to sea. Beyond the huddled cottages of the rest of the village Jenny glimpsed the signboard of the St. Cellan Arms swaying in the stiff breeze.

"Who was St. Cellan?"

"Some Celtic priest, I expect," said Guy. "I don't suppose many people around here know or care. They're all Methodists and go to an ugly little hall on the other side of the village."

"St. Cellan was a hermit," said Ted, "who lived in a stone house on the Downs and practiced faith healing."

"So Emma says. I don't believe a word of it."

Jenny said, "Who's Emma?"

"Emma St. Cellan. She and her brother Charles are the surviving members of an old local family."

"Ah yes, I remember you mentioning the surname before. Where do they live?"

"In a run-down barn of a house on the other side of the Downs. It's supposed to have been built on the original site of St. Cellan's holy cell."

"It's a fine house," said Ted, "or it would be if they had the money to maintain it properly."

"They'll never have the money."

"Emma told Dad the boutique's doing well."

"Maybe, but I suspect that what Emma makes at the boutique is hardly enough to keep her dressed in the latest fashions."

"What does her brother do?" Jenny asked idly.

"All kinds of things, but none of them for long. He used to dabble in motor racing and mountaineering, but after his father died and the Crown pocketed most of the inheritance in death duties Charles found he couldn't afford to go on living in that particular style, so he became a stuntman in films. I believe he did well for a while, but eventually he broke his neck—yes, literally!—and had to retire. At the moment he's probably looking around for something new to do. He's a partner in the Castlesea boutique, but boutiques aren't his line of country at all."

Once past the church the car had turned down a narrow street and now the wheels were bumping over a cart track which sloped around the side of the Downs towards the beach. The Cortina's speed was reduced to a crawl.

"Well, here we are," said Guy as Ted drove into the courtyard at the side of the house and halted the car outside a building which had once been a stable, "and there's Marguerite."

Marguerite had dressed with care and skill for the occasion. She wore a mustard-colored knitted suit, dark shoes too dainty to be fashionable but flattering to her narrow feet, and a tasteful gold brooch on the lapel of her jacket. Her hair, immaculately set, was just a dark enough brown to set off her complexion, the pink and white skin which had made her look anemic in adolescence and striking in maturity. As she came out of the house to meet them she moved with the confidence of a woman who was in her mid-forties but who could have passed for thirty-five.

"Guy!" she exclaimed warmly. "Oh, this is so exciting!" She kissed him on both cheeks. "I can't tell you how much we've all been looking forward to this . . . so this is Jenny! My dear, we've all been dying to see you! Welcome to Cellanporth!"

Jenny was at once smitten by an overpowering wave of shyness. She did manage to say "Thank you," but beyond that she was tongue-tied. She told herself that it was ridiculous to feel overwhelmed by Marguerite's appraising stare, but the more she told herself that it was ridiculous the more it seemed to her that Marguerite resembled a chatelain interviewing a new kitchen maid.

In fact, however, Marguerite was impressed. Good taste in clothes was her reaction, nice figure, I wonder if she has to diet, pity about the freckles, she can't know enough about makeup or she'd try to hide them, doesn't seem the fortune hunter type—or a grocer's daughter—I wonder how bad her accent is.

"Did you have a good journey?" she said sociably as she led them through the back door into a bright spacious kitchen. "When did you leave London?"

"Eleven o'clock," said Guy. "Yes, the journey went well. The train was on time for once."

"Did it rain?"

"It stopped when we reached Castlesea."

Oh, do be quiet, Guy, thought Marguerite. "Have you been to this part of the world before?" she said pointedly to Jenny.

"No," said the girl, blushing like a fourteen-year-old, and added in a rush, "It's beautiful. Guy never told me how beautiful it was."

A slight American accent, thought Marguerite with interest. Odd, of course, and rather a pity, but at least it was an improvement on the vowel sounds of the London suburbs. With luck she would lose the Americanisms in a year or two.

They were in the hall by this time. With a smile Marguerite opened the living room door and ushered Jenny across the threshold. "We all hope you'll enjoy your visit," she said kindly. "And now come and meet Guy's sister Anne."

4

There was little family resemblance between Guy and his sister. Anne had straight fair hair, which was drawn back from her face to trail down her back. She was slender, slight, ethereal—like a ghost, thought Jenny uneasily, or a refugee from some endless war. Anne's pallor made her face seem thinner than it was but the thinness accentuated the delicate bone structure of her face and emphasized the wide light eyes.

"Anne," said Guy, "this is Jenny."

"Yes, Roger explained all about her." Her voice was so natural that Jenny found it easy to smile and say "hullo" in what she hoped was a friendly voice. "Hullo," said Anne politely in response, and turned to the woman who was standing silently by the fireplace. "I'm going upstairs to my sitting room now, Grace. But you can stay down here if you want to."

The woman said, "We're all going to have tea down here, Anne. Don't you remember?"

Anne did not answer. She merely crossed the room and headed for the door where Guy was standing.

Guy said: "Won't you stay, Anne?" but when she ignored him he reluctantly stepped aside to let her pass.

Jenny heard Ted say quietly in the hall, "I'll have tea with you upstairs if you like, Anne."

But again Anne did not answer. The floorboards creaked lightly as she ran to the sanctuary of her room.

Grace Reid said crisply, "Excuse me, please," and disappeared after her; as silence closed upon the living room they all heard the slam of a door upstairs followed by the sound of furniture being dragged across the floor presumably to form a barricade.

"Oh *dear!*" said Marguerite, and looked profoundly embarrassed.

"Never mind," said Guy. "Grace will cope. Where's this promised tea, Marguerite? I'm damned hungry."

"Tea," said Marguerite mechanically. "Yes, of course. I'll go and get it ready straight away."

She left the room; they were alone. After a moment Jenny said hesitantly, "Why was Anne so afraid of me?"

"Oh, I'm sure there's no rational explanation." He opened the silver cigarette box which stood on the coffee table, but remembered just in time that he had forbidden himself to smoke. The lid clicked shut beneath the frustrated pressure of his fingertips. "At least she spoke to you normally enough. I was afraid she wouldn't even do that."

She wished he would smoke. She herself was longing for a cigarette but knew she could never light one when he so obviously wanted one himself.

"Don't worry, darling, she'll get used to you. Actually although you mightn't think it, that was a pretty good start. Don't let her behavior bother you too much."

"Guy!" called Ted purposefully from the hall. "Do you want me to help you bring in the suitcases?"

"No, that's all right, Ted, you don't have to do that."
He rose to his feet as he spoke and presently Jenny was
alone in that old-fashioned room with its low ceiling,
huge fireplace and sweeping view across the sands to the
sea.

To her disappointment she found later that the spare
room which Marguerite had prepared for them looked in
the other direction onto the steep slopes of the Downs
which towered directly behind the house. The Rectory
had five bedrooms; Anne used the master bedroom in the
front of the house as a private sitting room and slept in
the dressing room next door; Marguerite had the room on
the other side of the sitting room, and Ted had the room
next to his mother's, a corner room which not only faced
the sea but also overlooked the courtyard and the cart
track which led to the village. Grace's room, the
bathroom and the spare room, all faced the Downs.

Tea was finally served, but ended quickly when Grace
appeared to inform Guy that Anne had abandoned her
barricades and now wished to see him alone. While Guy
visited his sister Jenny had welcomed the chore of un-
packing as a chance to escape from Marguerite's thinly
veiled curiosity.

She had just changed into a pair of slacks and a
sweater and was stooping to close the last of the empty
suitcases, when Guy came into the room.

"Hullo," he said. "You look nice. How about a walk
along the beach? Dinner won't be for another hour so
there's plenty of time."

The idea of escaping to the beach was attractive. Guy
made no mention of his conversation with Anne, and
Jenny did not like to question him about it. For an uneasy
moment she was reminded of the days before they were

married when she had waited in vain for him to tell her the whole truth about Anne, but she tried to push the memory aside. So long as Anne was ill, Guy would feel guilty about her. In an effort to break the lengthening silence she said, "I didn't realize Grace the nurse was so young. I pictured her as fifty and matronly."

Guy laughed. "No, she's about my age. Everyone's been trying to marry her off to Roger for years—a marvelous idea except that neither Roger nor Grace regard it with any enthusiasm whatsoever."

Beyond the front gate there was a steep bank which separated them from the top of the beach. Guy gave her a helping hand as they scrambled down on to the sands, and then pulled her to him for a kiss.

"How are you standing up to this ordeal?"

"Ordeal—for heaven's sake!" It was easy for her to seem cheerful; she was so relieved that his preoccupation with Anne was forgotten. "It was much worse for you when I dragged you home to Balham!"

"But that was just for an afternoon!" He slipped an arm around her waist and when he kissed her again Jenny found she could even think of Marguerite's veiled condescension without qualms. Wandering with Guy across the beach she decided she must do her best to regard the enforced stay at the Rectory as a holiday instead of an uncomfortable visit to awkward in-laws.

"Let's hope the fine weather lasts," Guy was saying, unknowingly encouraging her in her efforts to believe they were on holiday, and began to point out some distant landmarks. To the south they could see the village of Cellanporth perched on top of the cliffs at the southern end of the bay; a few visitors were lingering on the sands near the path which led from the village to the beach, but they were all a long way away, toy figures against that vast landscape. To the north they could see the sand dunes which hid the estuary, harbor and cottages of Porthmawgan, and when Jenny glanced back over her shoulder she was confronted with the white-walled Rectory and the bare sloping humps of the Downs.

"The tide's coming in," said Guy presently.

The water was racing greedily across the sands toward them, and as they turned to wander south they were kept busy dodging the spurting tongues of surf.

"Look at those two people on horseback!" Jenny exclaimed suddenly. "Over there toward the cliffs—see? Don't they look unreal? I thought it was only in films that one saw beautiful horses being ridden along beautiful beaches . . . is it my imagination or are the riders really heading straight for us?"

There was a pause. "It's not your imagination," said Guy at last. "They are."

"Do you know them?"

"There are only two people in this part of the world who are capable of riding their horses along the shore like two stars in an epic movie." For a moment Jenny thought he wasn't going to say anything else but then he added casually, "Do you remember me talking in the car about the girl with the boutique in Castlesea and the brother who hurt his neck?"

Charles St. Cellan suddenly waved at them and spurred his horse to gallop the last few yards. Like Guy he was tall, dark and muscular; unlike Guy he had a full-lipped mouth, heavy-lidded eyes and a small but handsome white scar across his left cheekbone.

"What luck," Charles shouted. "We were hoping for a glimpse of you! How are you, old chap?" And he reined

in his horse so abruptly that the animal reared protestingly on its hind legs.

Just like a stuntman, thought Jenny fascinated as the
horse was brought under control and its rider slid deftly
from the saddle to stand beside them.

"Introduce me," said Charles, "to this gorgeous creature you're clutching so possessively. I suppose it's too
much to hope that she isn't your wife."

But before Guy could speak Emma joined them and
with the same dexterity as her brother reined in her horse
and dismounted. She wore white jeans, white riding boots
and a sweater of midnight blue. Black hair trailed care-
lessly to her shoulders; almond-shaped eyes and high
cheekbones gave her an unexpectedly oriental look.

"Hullo Guy," she said casually, and gave Jenny a cool
but not unfriendly smile. "Hi."

"Hi," murmured Jenny, responding automatically to
the Americanism, and then as the St. Cellans both eyed
her with a curiosity they made no attempt to hide, she
found to her fury that she was again tongue-tied with
shyness. Despite all her good resolutions her worries
came rushing back. The idea of being on holiday evapo-
rated; it seemed to her she was on trial again before a politely incredulous jury who were trying to convince themselves that Guy had had a logical reason for marrying her.
In panic she turned to Guy in the hope that he would say
something to divert their attention from her, but once
again Guy was given no chance to speak.

"Well, what's new, old chap?" Charles was saying
brightly. "Where have you been hiding yourself these last
few months? We heard from Leonard every time you
made a fleeting visit to Cellanporth to see Anne, but we

never even caught so much as a glimpse of you, did we, Emma? In fact we haven't set eyes on you since—"

"Charles," said his sister, "sometimes you're so tactless that I think your brain must be the size of a pea. Now is hardly the time to reminisce about when we last saw Guy." She turned to Jenny with a smile. "We were awfully pleased to hear Guy had got married again. How nice to have the opportunity of meeting you! I expect Guy's told you all about us, hasn't he?"

Jenny, already confused by the allusions to the past, was further confused by the direct question. "Why, yes," she answered, saying the first words to enter her head. "As a matter of fact we were talking about you both only this afternoon."

There was a second of silence broken only by the roar of the surf and the heavy breathing of Charles' horse. Heavens above, thought Jenny, what did I say? As she looked in confusion from Emma to Charles, Guy said to her in a quiet voice, "Jenny, we'll be late for dinner. We ought to start heading back to the Rectory."

"Hey, wait a minute!" Charles protested. "You can't just dash off like that after we've gone to all the trouble of riding along the beach in the hope of seeing you! How about inviting us in for a drink?"

"I'm just a guest at the Rectory," said Guy evenly. "It's Marguerite who issues the invitations. And now if you'll excuse us—"

"For God's sake!" exclaimed Charles annoyed. "What are you getting so tragically dignified about? Don't tell me that after all this time you're still harboring a grudge about something which wasn't our fault? Look, we want to bury the hatchet, don't we, Emma? We came down here hoping we would have a chance to congratulate you on your marriage and wish you well—"

"Thank you very much," said Guy. "I appreciate that. And now that you've satisfied your curiosity, which in fact was the only reason why you wanted to see me—"

"My dear chap, are you calling me a liar?"

"Don't be archaic, Charles," said Emma. "He knows damned well you're lying to the back teeth. If we'd wanted to see him for the reasons you gave we'd have driven to the Rectory and called on him in the conventional fashion and Guy's much too clever not to realize that. All right, Guy—you win. We wanted to see you and your wife out of sheer vulgar curiosity—there! Weren't we wicked! And now before you tell us to go to hell, can we invite you to visit us at Trecellan Hall some time during your stay?"

"Thanks, Emma, but we're going to be pretty busy while we're here. You'll have to excuse us. Come on, Jenny, we must be getting back."

"Why, you—" began Charles enraged but was interrupted by his sister.

"Shut up, Charles."

"But—"

"Shut *up*."

Guy was walking so fast that Jenny had difficulty keeping up with him. The clasp of his hand on hers was hot and tight and uncomfortable.

"Guy," she managed to say breathlessly at last, "Guy—"

"I'm sorry," he said. "I'm sorry but I just couldn't help it."

"—could you slow down a bit, please? My legs feel as though they're about to drop off."

He halted. She thought that at least he would smile, but to her dismay he merely pushed a harassed hand through his hair. "Sorry," he said again.

He seemed so distracted that she felt more upset than ever. She glanced back over her shoulder. The St. Cellans were standing by the water's edge, still staring after them, but as she watched she saw Emma mount her horse. Jenny thought, I mustn't ask him any questions, I mustn't cross-examine him. But the very next moment she heard herself say, "It was the St. Cellans who gave the party, wasn't it?"

And all Guy could say in reply was: "Yes—and I'm almost certain it was Charles who slipped Anne the LSD."

TWO

"God, what a bloody nerve!" said Charles.

"Mind the tide," said his sister from the safety of the saddle.

"How dare he brush us off like that!" Charles was so angry that he did not even notice the water swirling around his ankles.

"Oh God," said Emma with a yawn. "How childish men are sometimes. Charles, if Guy wants to appear white as driven snow, all I can say is good luck to him. What does it matter? Why should we mind if he wants to put on an act to impress his bride? Incidentally, what did you think of her?"

"I can't abide redheads," growled Charles.

"Liar! I thought she was rather sweet. Not at all Guy's type, though."

Charles had an aggravated awareness that it was he who should have made this last speech. "My dear girl, do you really have to put on such an unconvincing act of indifference? You know damned well you're just as angry with Guy as I am."

"Intrigued, yes," said Emma tranquilly. "Angry, no. What a splendid performance he gave! The stage has lost a great actor."

"And now, of course, his wife believes it was all our fault that Christina got killed and Anne went out of her mind!"

"Exactly," said Emma. "We're now the official scapegoats, but isn't it strange that after all this time Guy still feels he needs a scapegoat? Well, at least it proves one thing. You were right after all, Charles, and I was wrong."

"Right about what?"

"Right in thinking he hadn't told his new wife everything, of course. But who would ever have thought that Guy would be such a fool?"

THREE

Jenny's instinct was to say to Guy, "Why didn't you tell me before?" but she managed to suppress it. She was afraid that he would think she was nagging him, and besides the only answer he could possibly have made was the simple, "I didn't want to talk about it."

On their return to the Rectory he visited his sister again and Jenny, exhausted by the strain of the day, sank down on the spare-room bed in an unsuccessful attempt to rest.

The evening seemed long, even though Marguerite

went to bed before ten, and the night seemed longer. It rained; Jenny, lying in the dark, wondered depressed what they would do if it rained all day and confined them to the house, but by morning the sky was clear and the wind had dropped. While Guy was shaving Jenny leaned over the bedroom windowsill, savored the fresh air and watched the sheep browsing about her on the slopes of the Downs.

"Shall we go out this morning?" she said hopefully, and tried not to look too disappointed when Guy told her he wanted to talk to Roger again about Anne. The morning was further doomed when Guy discovered presently that he had left his traveler's checks behind at the flat in London and now had less than five pounds in his wallet.

"Are you sure you haven't lost the checks?"

"No, I put them on top of the stereo so that I couldn't forget them, but then I never went back into the living room. Never mind, I shouldn't have any difficulty cashing a check in Castlesea. Will you be all right on your own here for a few hours?"

"Oh yes." She had almost offered to go with him to Castlesea before she remembered that he would be calling on Roger for a private consultation. She tried to pull herself together. There was no reason why she shouldn't enjoy the morning exploring the beach even if she went alone. When he left soon after breakfast she decided to avoid the temptation to sit and mope. Making a great effort she returned to the dining room, stacked the breakfast plates and took them into the kitchen to wash them up.

"No, no, I wouldn't dream of letting you do that!" Marguerite, who always breakfasted punctually at seven-thirty before settling down to her bath and manicure, was by this time seated at the kitchen table while she made her shopping list. A cup of coffee steamed beside her to stimulate her memory. "Mrs. Evans, my daily help, will be here in a minute and she always does the breakfast things. . . . Besides, you're on holiday. Relax and enjoy yourself, dear."

She made Jenny feel exactly like a child told to run along and amuse itself for an hour or two. Jenny flushed, her anger at Marguerite's tone mingling with her relief at the chance to escape from her company. She was just heading toward the front door when Grace Reid came briskly down the stairs.

"Good morning." They both spoke at once, and afterwards both laughed.

"Where did Guy go?" asked Grace. "I saw him drive off in the Cortina five minutes ago."

Jenny explained about the checks.

"Oh, I see," said Grace. She smoothed her hands quickly over her gray skirt and fidgeted with the button of her cardigan.

"How is Anne this morning?" asked Jenny, anxious to escape but equally anxious not to seem impolite.

"Not bad." Grace was laconic, as if Anne were suffering from a cold. Looking at her closely for the first time Jenny was struck by the determined set of Grace's face; the jaw was square, the eyebrows were straight and thick and the eyes were iron-gray. It was a masculine face, and the curling urchin cut of her hair hardly made it more feminine.

"Well, you'll excuse me—"

"Yes, of course." The iron-gray eyes regarded her with interest. "What a smart trouser suit you're wearing, if you don't mind me saying so. Did you buy it in New York?"

"Yes, I did. Last autumn."

"I thought of going to America myself at one time. Did you work there?"

"Yes, before I was married, but afterwards . . . well, I probably should have got a job, but—"

"Oh heavens," said Grace, "why work if you don't have to? That's what money's for, isn't it? To stop you doing a lot of things you don't want to be bothered with?"

"I suppose so," said Jenny, and added with the vague idea of being tactful, "But sometimes it can be unsatisfying not to work."

"Oh, I'm all for people working if they want to, but a lot of people don't want to. Guy, for instance."

"Oh," said Jenny. "Guy." The sudden introduction of his name came as a shock.

"He was always moaning about how bored he was with being an architect. Well, I mustn't waste your time by gossiping like this. Is Mrs. Stratton in the kitchen?"

"Yes," said Jenny blankly, and the next moment found herself alone in the hall.

Opening the front door she stepped out into the cool morning air and moved slowly down the flagstone path to the little gate above the beach. Grace's casual remark about Guy had disturbed her; she remembered that Guy had once mentioned to her how bored he was with designing skyscrapers, but it had been such a lighthearted remark that she hadn't given it a second thought. He certainly hadn't "moaned" to her about his job. He had been annoyed that he had not been able to take more time off for the honeymoon, but no more than seemed natural.

"Jenny!"

She jumped. Spinning around she saw that Ted was strolling down the path toward her.

"You were miles away!" he said with a smile. "That was the third time I'd called your name. What were you thinking about?"

"Nothing special. I'd decided to go for a walk, but as you can see I didn't get very far."

"Do you want to come to Cellanporth with me? I'm working at my father's pub this vacation, and I promised I'd go over there this morning to help him with a shipment from the brewery. My father would like to meet you."

Jenny welcomed the distraction. "Can we walk across the beach?"

"Yes, that's quicker. We can go up the cliff path and come out right at the pub." He held the gate open for her and helped her scramble down the path to the beach. "Besides," he added as an afterthought, "I like to walk by the sea."

For some reason she felt relaxed in his company. Perhaps it was because he was only a year younger than she was.

"Do you go out much on your father's boat?" she asked presently.

"Never, I get seasick. But so long as I'm on dry land I love the water."

"It must be wonderful to live here all the year round."

"Yes, I hate to go away to Bristol each term."

"What are you reading there?"

"Engineering."

"Do you like it?"

"It's okay."

Jenny watched the wheeling of the gulls over the beach,.

and as she drew closer to the cliffs she noticed the sheep grazing on the grassy headland far above the sands.

"Is it an optical illusion," she asked at last, "or are those sheep really as close to the edge of the cliff as I think they are?"

"They do go near the edge. Sometimes they even fall over and you get a smelly corpse on the beach until the sea washes it away. Sheep are such silly animals."

They were close enough by this time to see the caves at the foot of the cliffs, the rocky inlets hewn by a million years of corroding tides. Ted turned aside.

"This way," he said. "The path's at the back of the beach. Incidentally, I hope you're in good training."

"Heavens, are you going to rope us together?"

He smiled at her. "It's not as bad as that, but it's quite a haul."

Jenny soon decided that this was an understatement. She spent the next fifteen minutes concluding that she was in poor physical condition.

"This is what my mother ought to do every day," said Ted as they paused halfway up for a rest. "Then she wouldn't have to diet all the time."

"Um," said Jenny, too breathless to say anything else.

They started to climb again, and at last the path reached the road which ended at the pub. Jenny paused to catch her breath. She had her back to the old stone walls of the St. Cellan Arms; to her left the road meandered past the church and the huddled cottages of the village, and ahead of her was a field, now empty, which was evidently used as a car park for the pub's customers as well as the tourists who came out for the day. To her right stretched the long arm of the headland which plunged down toward the sea before rearing up again to form the Snake's Tail, and just past the pub at the beginning of the footpath stood a large white board bearing the warning:

> THESE CLIFFS ARE DANGEROUS.
>
> DO NOT GO NEAR THE EDGE.
>
> DO NOT LET CHILDREN
>
> WANDER FROM PATH.

Beyond the notice board, in blissful ignorance of all danger, the group of sheep were still browsing on the sloping edge of the precipice.

"Silly animals," said Ted again, and led the way around the side of the pub to the back door.

There was no one in the untidy kitchen, but in the public bar they found Leonard reading the racing section of the *Daily Express*. He was sitting on the window seat with his feet resting on one of the small tables and a cigarette drooping from the corner of his mouth.

"Morning, Dad. I've brought you a visitor."

Leonard dropped his newspaper, hauled his feet off the table and removed his cigarette all within the space of three seconds.

"Hullo love," he said. "I was just wondering when you were going to do me the honor of a visit. Where's his lordship?"

"Who?" said Jenny confused.

"Mr. G. Stratton."

"Oh, Guy! He had to go into Castlesea."

"What a bloody funny thing to have to do on a morning like this to a girl like you." He stuck out his hand, took hers firmly and shook it. "How about a spot of tea?"

Here again was someone with whom she could feel at ease. She smiled. "Well, I don't want to put you to any trouble—"

"Ted can be put to the trouble. Put the kettle on, Ted. Sit down, love, that's right, make yourself comfortable. Well, what does England seem like after America? Bloody dull, I'll bet."

"No, kind of peaceful really, Mr.—"

"Leonard. You've got an American accent."

Jenny blushed. "It's difficult not to pick up a few inflections and phrases," she began defensively, but Leonard only laughed and told her frankly that he liked it. "We get some Americans down here sometimes," he added placidly. "I always charge them twice as much because I don't want them to feel they're not at home. Very hospitable we are here to Americans . . . Cigarette?"

"Thank you."

He gave her a light. He had large strong brown hands and the nails of his fingers were square and dirty. His eyes with their amused ironical expression were bright blue in his tanned face, and his gray hair, crinkled and tousled, looked as though he had forgotten to comb it that morning. He wore a pair of patched trousers, a fishermen's-knit sweater which might once have been beige, and a pair of tartan socks.

"How are you getting on, Ted?" he shouted in the direction of the kitchen. "Can you find the teapot?"

"I'm just rinsing it out."

"That's my boy," said Leonard comfortably, and

swung his feet back onto the table again. "Let's see, where were we? Oh yes, America. You met Guy in New York, didn't you?"

"Yes, ages ago," Jenny said readily, and added on an impulse, "I was friends with Christina."

"Oh," said Leonard, and to her astonishment she saw that he was at a loss for a reply. Recovering he added casually, "Wouldn't have thought you were Christina's type somehow, love."

"Well, I wasn't really, but we were next-door neighbors and often went on shopping expeditions together."

"Oh," said Leonard blankly again.

"Did you know Christina well?" Jenny said in a rush.

"Yes and no. She and Guy didn't come down here much, but on the couple of occasions when they did I felt I'd known her as long as I'd known Guy. . . ." Leonard blew a smoke ring at the ceiling. "It was the hell of a shock when she got herself killed like that. Horrible business, falling over the bloody cliff—" He stopped. "For Christ's sake! Didn't Guy tell you that?"

It took Jenny several seconds to reply. Amidst the intensity of the shock she was aware for the first time that Guy had never told her exactly how Christina died; he had talked of the beach, talked of the body being sodden and covered with sand, and had left her to draw her own false conclusions.

At last she managed to say levelly, "I'm sorry . . . something Guy said . . . I was under the impression she was drowned."

"Well, she was washed up on the beach all right, but the general medical opinion was—hey, you don't want to talk about this. My God, Guy goes to all the trouble not to upset you too much and I come along and screw up all his good work! I'm sorry. Look, have some—where *is* that tea? Ted! What are you doing out there? Is the kettle on?"

"Coming! Give me a chance, can't you?"

"But Leonard," Jenny heard herself say. "Leonard—"

"Yes, love?"

Jenny's anger at this latest example of Guy's failure to confide in her was fast being overtaken by feelings of bewildered disbelief. "I can see Christina being drowned if she took an impulsive swim and got swept onto the rocks by the current," she heard herself say in a rapid, uneven voice. "I mean, that sort of thing often happens in this part of the world, doesn't it? But how could Christina possibly have fallen over the cliff?"

"Well, it was a party, you see, love, and a lot of people weren't quite themselves, if you follow me. Of course no one in their right mind goes dancing along the edge of a cliff in the dark, but you know what parties are."

"Yes, but—"

"Don't worry, love, the coroner rejected the idea that anyone might have pushed her."

In the silence that followed Ted called, "Dad, where's the sugar?"

"Under the sink!"

There was another pause.

At last Jenny said, "Pushed her?"

"Don't take any notice of me, love—I always say these wild things, it must be my love of the dramatic. . . . My God, here's the bloody tea! And about time too, if I may

say so, Ted Matthews. Now, Mrs. S., how do you like
your tea—milk alone, milk with sugar, sugar alone or just
plain naked?"

Afterwards she decided it was then that she first started
to feel frightened.

5

ONE

The lorry from the brewery arrived before Leonard had
touched his tea, and he and Ted went outside to help un-
load. Left on her own in the bar Jenny abandoned her
cup and slipped outside through the small untended garden to the little gate which led out onto the cliffs.

She was thinking of Guy, of course, wondering how
many other secrets he had kept from her. He had felt
guilty she told herself. Guilty about Anne—yes, she could
understand that. But guilty about Christina?

Jenny stopped abruptly. She found she was face to face
again with the warning notice and was struck afresh by
the bareness of the headland. She saw that short grass
clinging to the soil, the clumps of heather mingled with the
banks of gorse, and presently she glanced across the bay
to the distant dunes which fringed Porthmawgan. When
she moved beyond the notice she saw at once why the

cliffs were so dangerous. There was no immediate sheer drop to the beach. Instead the ground sloped at first gradually and then with increasing steepness to a precipice some yards away. How easy to wander along the top of the slope, how easy to catch one's foot in the heather, stumble, lose one's balance, roll over and over toward the edge . . .

Ted's voice said behind her, "We've finished the unloading and the beer's all in the cellar. Dad wants to know if you'd like another cup of tea."

But Jenny no longer felt sociable. "It's very kind of your father," she said awkwardly and made a great business of glancing at her watch. "But I think I should be getting back. Guy'll be home soon. Will you be staying on here?"

To her dismay Ted shook his head. "No, I told Mother I'd be back at the Rectory for lunch—officially I don't have to start work until five-thirty. I'll come back with you."

Fortunately he said little on the return journey and Jenny tried to decide what she should say to Guy. She knew she should tread carefully since the subject was such a delicate one, but she was beginning to feel that she would be justified in showing a trace of annoyance. It was not until they were halfway across the beach that she realized with a mixture of dread and panic that she was afraid not of Guy but of what evasion she might discover next.

It was noon when they reached the Rectory. Marguerite had borrowed Grace's small Austin to drive to the village and since there was no sign of the Cortina Jenny realized Guy still had not returned from Castlesea. At first she was relieved that the confrontation was to be postponed, but presently the relief faded and she was aware only of her increasing tension as she followed Ted through the kitchen into the hall. She was just wondering what she should do next to pass the time when a door opened upstairs and Grace came running downstairs to meet them.

"Ah, there you are, Ted. I wonder if you could sit with Anne for a few minutes? I've just realized that the supply of one set of pills is very low—I thought there was another bottle in the medicine cupboard but there isn't, so I want to run over to Roger's to get an emergency supply. I can't go over to the chemist because there's no car here at the moment."

"That's all right," said Ted. "I'll sit with her."

Jenny had followed Ted upstairs with the vague idea that she might change into a dress when the sound of a car engine made her run to the bedroom window. Leaning out over the sill she saw to her amazement a very old, very dignified Rolls Royce. It was in immaculate condition. Black paint shone, chromium gleamed and on the door of the driver's seat a psychedelic flower flared a brilliant pink in the midday sunlight.

The door swung open and Emma St. Cellan, exotic in black boots, black sweater and scarlet tunic, sprang out, flicked back a strand of hair from her eyes and strolled across the courtyard toward the back door.

Jenny's heart sank. Emma was the last person she wanted to see. On an impulse she hurried to the landing in search of moral support. "Ted!"

"Yes?" The door of Anne's sitting room was closed so that his voice sounded muffled, but she heard his footsteps and the next moment he was facing her across the threshold. "What is it?"

"Emma St. Cellan's here." Jenny tried to deliver the information nonchalantly so that Ted would think all responsibility for the unexpected visitor was passed to him, but unfortunately he failed to take the hint.

"Oh God," he said with a grimace. "Well, let Mother deal with her."

"She's not back yet," objected Jenny, trying to remain nonchalant and not succeeding. "Neither's Guy. Or Grace."

"Oh . . . Well, just tell Emma that no one's at home and I expect she'll go away." And he dived back into the room to rejoin Anne.

Damn, thought Jenny. She knew it was unreasonable of her to be so upset but she had a strong intuition that a further interview with Emma could only spell trouble. She began to tiptoe toward her room but a board creaking beneath her feet made Emma call, "Guy? Is that you?"

Jenny made an enormous effort to pull herself together. "No, Guy's out," she called, surprising herself by sounding very calm, and marched firmly to the head of the stairs.

"Ah, good morning!" exclaimed Emma with a welcoming smile. "How nice to see you! The back door was unlatched but I was beginning to think the house was deserted. Is Charles here?"

"Charles?" said Jenny blankly.

"My brother. The exhibitionist I was with when we all met yesterday evening on the beach." Emma was wandering into the living room and tossing her gloves onto the coffee table. "He was going to come over here across the Downs—it's only a twenty-minute walk if you don't go around by the road. I gave him a good start and then left in the Rolls. But obviously the start I gave him wasn't good enough."

"No, he's not here yet."

"Never mind." Emma glanced in the mirror above the fireplace and adjusted her hair. "By the way I do hope you don't mind us calling on you, but we were both so anxious to see you again and since Guy said you'd be too busy to come to Trecellan Hall we thought our only hope was to visit the Rectory . . . where is Guy, by the way?"

"In Castlesea." Jenny did her best to appear as self-possessed as her guest. "Marguerite and Grace are in Cellanporth and Ted's upstairs with Anne. Can I offer you a drink?"

"Sweet of you," said Emma. "I'll have a gin and tonic."

"I'm not sure where they keep the gin. Excuse me a minute." Jenny hurried to the dining room, discovered the gin under the sideboard and retreated to the kitchen in search of a glass and a bottle of tonic. When she returned to the living room she found Emma sitting on the sofa and smoking a very long cigarette.

"Now do tell me," said Emma, "how are you enjoying being Mrs. Guy Stratton?"

"Very much, thank you. Do you want some ice in this?"

"No, thanks—that looks lovely. But aren't you having one too?"

"Drinking in the middle of the day makes me sleepy." Jenny sat down on the edge of one of the armchairs and tried to look relaxed.

"Well, here's to you," said Emma kindly. "And now that we're alone together, may I say a very special word of congratulations to you on hooking such an attractive man. I was always one of Guy's biggest fans, you know, so you must forgive me if I sound a bit envious! But seriously, Charles and I like Guy a lot, so we were both a bit devastated when he brushed us off on the beach yesterday."

"I'm sure Guy didn't mean——"

"Oh, but he did! That was painfully obvious. In fact, that was another reason why we decided to call on you—we both felt we simply had to straighten things out. You see, those ghastly tragedies simply weren't our fault. I know we gave the party, but—Guy did tell you about the party, didn't he?"

"Oh yes," said Jenny. She was trying to think of an excuse to leave the room.

"Then he'll have told you how Charles paid a lot of attention to Anne and it's true—he did. But Charles didn't give Anne the LSD, so there's simply no sense in Guy blaming him for all her troubles."

"I see," said Jenny. She was straining her ears for the sound of a car.

"And as for Christina—well, how could Charles and I have been responsible? She was always getting stoned—it was just our luck that she was at our party when she had the frightful accident. The plain fact of the matter is that if anyone's responsible for what happened it's Guy himself—and it really wasn't his fault. It would have been just too Victorian if he had refused to let either of his women out of his sight, and besides . . . well, it would be hypocritical of me to blame Guy for ignoring his wife and sister when I did my very best to make him forget them."

There was a pause. The silence was broken only by the wind humming in the eaves and the distant drone of the sea. Jenny was aware of her heart thumping rapidly against her ribs.

"You knew, of course," said Emma, "that I was Guy's mistress."

There was only one answer to that. "Of course," said Jenny. She felt sick. She did not dare move for fear the nausea would overcome her so remained where she was, willing Emma to leave.

But Emma was enjoying herself too much. "I was sorry it didn't last longer," she was saying dreamily. "He's marvelous in bed—but I don't have to tell you that, do I! I say, are you sure you won't have a drink? This is awfully good gin."

Rage suddenly swept through Jenny. "If you'll excuse me," she said springing to her feet, "I really don't have the time to listen to—"

"Of course—I'm sorry, I'm probably interrupting all sorts of plans you've made for this morning! Don't worry about me. I think I'll pop upstairs and say hullo to Ted and Anne—you did say they were at home, didn't you?"

Jenny just managed to nod.

"Fine! I'll look in on them until Charles arrives." And before Jenny could say another word, Emma had finished her drink and was moving languidly into the hall.

Jenny returned to the dining room, excavated the gin and mixed herself a stiff drink. Her hands were shaking, though whether from shock, anger, humiliation or pain she hardly knew. She wanted Guy to come back but was suddenly terrified he would think she was making a fuss about nothing. After all, she had known he hadn't always been faithful to Christina . . .

Jenny shivered.

She had wandered back to the living room, her hands still gripping her glass and now as she glanced out of the window she saw Charles St. Cellan standing on the bank above the beach some yards to the left of the house. His appearance, like his sister's, held a touch of the exotic; he wore a lime-green sweater with a white rolled collar and white cuffs, and his purple corduroy slacks clung snugly to his slim hips. The wind was blowing his dark hair into his eyes, but as Jenny watched he tossed his head to clear his vision and began to wander casually along the top of the bank toward the little front gate.

Jenny set down her glass and hurried out into the hall. The door of Anne's sitting room was open; as she mounted the stairs to tell Emma of Charles' arrival Jenny could clearly hear every word that was being said.

"Ah, there's Charles," Emma was observing. "He certainly took his time about getting here. Well, it's been nice seeing you again, Anne—" She broke off.

The silence which followed was so intense that Jenny stopped automatically.

"What is it, Anne?" asked Ted urgently. "What's the matter?"

There was another silence, and then as Jenny remained frozen on the stairs Anne cried out in fear, "He killed her! He's the one! He killed her!" And after that there was no sound at all except for Anne's quick frightened breathing.

TWO

Emma said abruptly, "Nonsense, Anne, Charles wouldn't

harm a fly!" A succession of small sounds indicated she was preparing to leave.

Without pausing to think why she should want to conceal her presence, Jenny tiptoed up the remaining stairs and darted behind the half-open door of her bedroom.

Ted was saying to Emma, "Take him away from here, can't you? Take him away, for God's sake!" And as Emma emerged from the sitting room Jenny heard him add gently to Anne: "It's all right—they're both going. Don't worry. It's all right."

Emma had just reached the head of the stairs when Charles called idly from the hall, "Anyone at home?"

"Charles!" She began to run downstairs. "Charles, the most extraordinary thing's happened! Quick, let's go. Through the kitchen—come on—"

"But my dear girl, I've only just arrived!"

"Come *on,* Charles!"

"But . . ." His voice trailed away protestingly as he allowed her to led him to the back door.

There was a silence. Leaning over the windowsill again Jenny saw the Rolls turn with difficulty in the confined space of the courtyard and sway up the cart track to the village. For some minutes she remained motionless. Then, hurrying from the room, she found Ted lingering by the stairs.

"Did you hear that?" he asked her abruptly.

"I—"

"No, I suppose you couldn't have done if you were in your room."

Jenny certainly had no wish to admit to eavesdropping. "What happened?"

"Anne looked out of the window, saw Charles St. Cellan and said he was a murderer."

"Good heavens!" she exclaimed, wondering if she was overdoing the astonishment, but Ted showed no sign of suspicion. "What an extraordinary thing to happen!"

"That's an understatement." His fingers smoothed the polished wood of the bannisters. "Did you see Charles?"

Jenny remembered just in time that Charles had approached the house from the front. "No, I didn't," she said rapidly, "but I knew he was coming. Emma said he was on his way. But Ted, about Anne——"

"She said: 'He——' meaning Charles '——killed her.' But that doesn't make any sense. Killed who? Christina? But nobody killed Christina. She was just freaked out, thought she could fly and jumped off the cliff trying to prove it. That's what everyone said at the inquest. Besides, why on earth would Charles want to kill Christina? He'd only met her a couple of times."

"Did Anne say anything after Emma left?" asked Jenny.

"No, she hasn't spoken a word. I wish to God Grace would come back."

Far away downstairs the back door closed.

"Grace?" yelled Ted.

Footsteps rang out across the kitchen floor.

"Guy!" cried Jenny, and despite all her recent resentment she ran down the stairs to meet him.

"Yes, it's me at last—sorry I took so long." He noticed nothing unusual; there was no hesitation before he kissed her. "Grace is just coming," he called upstairs to Ted. "I passed her in the village and gave her a lift but it's lucky we're still alive to tell the tale. We nearly had a head-on collision with the St. Cellans in the high street. I can't think why Charles always has to drive as if he's competing in the Monte Carlo rally. . . ." He was drifting into the dining room as he spoke. "Can I get you a drink before lunch, darling?"

"No, not now." Her nervousness about confronting him had vanished, she realized. The scene she had overheard between Anne and Emma had jolted aside her timidity and left only an overwhelming desire to learn the truth. "Guy, about the St. Cellans—"

"Yes?"

"They were here. At the Rectory."

He swung around. As the expression in his eyes changed she closed the dining room door and leaned back against the panels. "They arrived separately—Emma in their car and Charles on foot. Emma arrived first. She went to see Anne and while she was upstairs in the sitting room Charles arrived. Anne looked out of the window, saw Charles and cried out in a terrified voice: 'He killed her!' "

"What! Are you sure?" Guy looked more appalled that stunned. "Where were you—in the room?"

"No, but the door was open and I overheard her. She was with Ted. We both heard her—ask him."

"She must have been hallucinating." He was attempting a quick recovery but Jenny saw he was very shaken. As she watched he turned to the sideboard, reached for a glass and poured himself some scotch. "There's no other explanation."

"Why are you so sure? Guy—" Her nerve failed her at last. She stopped.

He drank half the scotch in his glass before facing her again. "Why am I so sure?" he repeated at last in a tired bitter voice. "Because I've known beyond any shadow of doubt for a very long time that it was Anne herself who killed Christina."

THREE

"She was out of her mind at the time," Guy said heavily at last. "She probably thought Christina was threatening her in some way. There must have been a struggle up there on the cliffs and when Christina missed her footing—"

Jenny's concern for him was at once diverted. The memory of Leonard's information about Christina's death stirred her anger again. "Guy, why on earth did you never tell me about those cliffs?"

He looked blank. "I did tell you."

"You most certainly did not! You gave me the impression she drowned. You told me—"

"I told you I found her on the beach."

"You never told me how she got there! I heard about that this morning from Leonard Matthews and I felt such a fool for being so ignorant."

"I'm sorry," he said, and he sounded so subdued, so genuinely repentant, that her anger at once subsided. "I'm very sorry. I thought I . . . no, I knew I hadn't told you. But my decision to avoid telling you if possible was linked with my fear for Anne. I was so afraid you might put two and two together—"

"But Guy, you must have realized I would find out what happened to Christina!"

"Why should you have done? Maybe I was naive but I thought people usually had better taste than to speak to a man's second wife about her predecessor, particularly when the predecessor was a woman like Christina. . . . However, I might have known Leonard wouldn't bother about good taste." He sighed and made a brief helpless gesture with his hands. "And besides—"

"Yes?"

"I wanted to believe she'd drowned," he said rapidly. "I didn't see how Anne could possibly have drowned her. But the cliffs . . . and those cliffs are dangerous . . . Anne needn't have used much force—"

Jenny pounced on the hypothetical tone of this last statement. "You've no proof Anne pushed her, have you? It's only supposition?"

"My God," said Guy, "I wish it was. No, Anne had definitely been in a struggle. Her clothes were torn and her face was scratched and a fragment of her dress was found still clutched in Christina's hand. A thread was trapped under the fingernail."

"But didn't the police find that?"

"No, because I discovered the body and the first thing I did was to remove any evidence which incriminated Anne."

Jenny was struck dumb. She understood now exactly why Guy had been so secretive, and as soon as she understood she wished that understanding still eluded her. Covering up a possible murder . . . When she was able to speak again all she could say was, "Does anyone else know about this?"

"Only Ted—he was with me at the time, but he won't say anything. He wants to protect Anne. So does Roger Carpenter, who's more than a little in love with her, and I'm sure Roger suspects the truth although we've never come right out and discussed it. Marguerite probably has her suspicions too, but she's content to stay on the sidelines and avoid trouble. A lot of people must have had their suspicions, but there was no proof. When I destroyed that evidence, I didn't know that Anne was seriously ill. All I could think was that Anne had killed Christina and I couldn't bear the thought of her being taken into custody, standing trial at Castlesea—or even the Old Bailey—being sentenced to prison. . . . Of course now I know she'd be judged unfit to plead, but she'd still be sent to a hospital for the criminally insane. Anne—in a place like that! I'd have done anything to prevent that happening to her, anything at all." He paused, but Jenny said nothing. "Darling—" He moved to her and she could sense his tension and anxiety. "—darling, please try to understand. I know what I did was strictly against the law, but what would you have done if you'd been in my shoes? Just what in God's name would you have done?"

"Well, I . . ." But it was no use. She no longer wanted to oppose him. She was about to tell him so when without warning Grace Reid entered the room.

"Guy—oh, excuse me." On seeing them deep in conversation she prepared to retreat again but Guy raised a hand to stop her.

"What is it, Grace?"

"I was only going to tell you that I thought I'd phone Roger and ask him to come over. Did you hear what happened?"

"Yes, Jenny told me."

"Odd, wasn't it?" Grace looked disturbed. "I suppose it must have been a hallucination. Anyway, I think Roger should see Anne as soon as possible. She's very upset."

"Do you want me to phone him?"

"No, I'll do it. I just thought you should know about the St. Cellans, that's all." And she withdrew as abruptly as she had arrived.

Guy swirled the scotch around with an absentminded

movement of his hand. "How did the St. Cellans react to Anne's remark?" he asked Jenny suddenly.

"Well, Charles wasn't in the room but Emma was obviously astounded. She left almost at once, collared Charles in the hall and propelled him out of the house as quickly as possible. I remember she started off by saying, 'Charles, the most extraordinary thing has happened.'"

"Hm." Guy was still toying with his drink. "Why the devil did the St. Cellans come here anyway? It surely wasn't just idle curiosity—they must have been well satisfied on the sands yesterday when they saw you face to face."

"I think they wanted to pay you back for that brush-off you gave them."

"Oh?" His expression changed. "Why? What did Emma say?"

"Oh, nothing much." Some strange reaction was making her eerily self-possessed. "She just wanted to tell me how wonderful you were in bed, but of course I knew that already."

Guy was speechless. Before he could even think of replying the door opened without warning for the second time and Marguerite's high heels clicked across the polished floorboards. "Ah, there you are!" she exclaimed cheerfully. "I was wondering where you'd both got to. I'm afraid lunch will be a little late because I was delayed in the village—I simply had to pop in and see Mrs. Evans' new grandchild—but everything should be ready in about twenty minutes. Am I interrupting anything if I start to set the table?"

"Let me do it," offered Jenny, still so unnaturally calm

that she sounded almost gay. "I've been far too idle since I arrived."

"Well, that's very nice of you, dear . . ." Marguerite handed her a tablecloth and showed her where the cutlery was. "Thank you so much." And her high heels clicked across the floor again toward the kitchen.

Guy closed the dining room door. "Are you angry with me?" he said at last in a low voice.

"Angry? Oh no! I knew you had had affairs while you were married to Christina."

Her calmness now sounded hideously false. She turned away abruptly.

After a moment Guy said, "So you *are* angry."

"Well, for God's sake, you don't expect me to be thrilled about it, do you?" She was trying not to cry.

"It was Christina who had the affairs," said Guy at last. "I had no affairs, just a series of one-night stands to try to convince myself I could satisfy other women even if I couldn't satisfy my wife. And that was all my relationship was with Emma. A one-night stand. If it hadn't been completely meaningless I would have told you about it."

For a second Jenny felt herself back in New York, back at the Stratton parties, back in a world where people slept with one another as casually as they shook hands. A coldness settled on her. She said nothing.

"Jenny, Emma means nothing to me. Nothing at all."

"I know." She did her best to blink back her tears and be sensible. "I'm sorry, I don't mean to be stupid about this but—"

"But?"

"I hated hearing about it from her!" Jenny burst out.

"I wouldn't have minded a bit if you'd told me yourself—
well, perhaps I would have minded, but to hear it from
her . . . it—it was horrible. I hated her for telling me and
I hated you for not telling me and I hated myself for hat-
ing you."

"My poor darling. I'm sorry. Here." He tilted her chin
upwards and kissed her. Anger died as her resistance
ebbed; he drew her closer to him and slid his hands slowly over her hips.

"Am I forgiven?"

Jenny felt that it should not have been so easy for her
to say yes, but she said it just the same. Guy began to kiss
her again, and her relief at being close to him again made
it easy to tell herself that nothing mattered so long as
Guy loved her. When he suggested that they should go to
their room it never occurred to her to say no.

They slipped upstairs. Marguerite, busying herself in
the kitchen, did not hear them and by the time she returned to the dining room and found to her exasperation
that the table had not been set. Guy had already
smoothed away the last of Jenny's doubts in the bed he
had once shared with Christina.

FOUR

Guy seemed determined to compensate Jenny for her unfortunate morning by paying her as much attention as
possible. After lunch he offered to take her for a drive.
The weather had become more erratic, but Jenny did not
mind; it was enough for her simply to be alone with him.
At one point Guy stopped so that they could get out and
walk along the cliffs, but the wind was strong enough to

make each step a battle and when the rain began to sting their faces they hurried back to the car.

By the time they returned to the Rectory it was five o'clock and the house was quiet. A friend had given Marguerite a lift into the village to attend a women's institute meeting; Ted had already left for work.

"Perhaps everyone's out," Jenny murmured as Guy led the way upstairs.

To prove her wrong the door of Anne's sitting room opened and Grace came out to welcome them.

"There was a phone call for you, Guy," she said. "I've no idea who it was because she wouldn't leave a name. Said she'd ring again later."

"How odd," said Guy. "I wonder who that could have been."

"Someone from your office perhaps?"

"Perhaps. Did she have a slight Yorkshire accent?"

"No, definitely not." Grace frowned. "Mid-Atlantic, if anything—the sort of accent a lot of people like to assume nowadays. But I could be mistaken. She hardly said more than half a dozen words."

"All right, thanks, Grace. I suppose I'll just have to curb my curiosity and wait for her to phone again."

The telephone started to ring.

"That's a coincidence," said Guy lightly, and ran downstairs to the living room phone.

Jenny hauled herself up the remaining stairs and wandered across the landing to their bedroom. By the time Guy came back she was brushing her hair which the wind had whipped into a tangle and gritting her teeth as the bristles dragged at the knots.

"Who was it?" she said idly, glancing at him in the mirror.

"My boss's secretary. I'd forgotten she had a vague American inflection." He unzipped his windbreaker and eased off his shoes. "It was nothing important."

"That's good." Jenny untangled the last knot, abandoned the hairbrush and leaned forward toward the mirror to examine her makeup.

The wind dropped after dinner and a pale moon sailed serenely in a clear sky. Jenny was tempted to suggest a stroll along the deserted beach but to her surprise Guy said he wanted to have an early night.

"Stay up for a while if you like," he said quickly, sensing her disappointment. "There's no reason why you should have an early night if you don't want one."

But Jenny had no wish to be left alone with Marguerite. "No, I think I'll come to bed too. Would it disturb you if I read for a while?"

"Not in the least."

But later when they were both in bed and Jenny was reaching for her book he said lightly, "Do you really want to read?"

"Not if it'll disturb you."

"I'm already disturbed. I'll never be able to sleep if I know I can open my eyes and see you propped up on the pillows solemnly reading *Anna Karenina*."

She laughed. "That doesn't sound very sexy!"

He laughed too and reached over to turn out her light. "Why go to bed with a book when you're already in bed with your husband?"

"I thought you were having an early night because you were so tired!"

"I've made a stunning recovery. Anyway I didn't really want an early night—that was just the best excuse I could think of to avoid sitting around downstairs watching television with Marguerite."

"That makes two of us—how awful we are! Poor Marguerite!"

"Forget Marguerite. Forget Anna Karenina. Forget everyone."

And Jenny forgot.

She was never certain what awoke her later. The luminous dial of her alarm clock told her it was twenty past ten, and Marguerite had by that time been in bed for nearly an hour. Grace and Anne had both retired for the night; the house was in darkness and would remain so until Ted returned from his father's pub between eleven-thirty and midnight.

Jenny was about to shift her position when she felt Guy stir beside her.

He was slipping silently out of bed, and because his movements were unmistakably furtive Jenny remained motionless, watching him in bewilderment through her lashes. She saw him grope by the chair where he had left his clothes; the next moment he had padded noiselessly from the room, his clothes in his arms, to dress in the bathroom.

She waited for him to come back, but he did not. After a moment the bathroom door clicked open again, and she heard the creak of the floorboard as he moved to the head of the stairs.

She was out of bed almost before she realized it. Her feet carried her out onto the landing just in time to hear the rasp of the Yale lock far away in the hall and a second later the front door was pulled shut. He was gone. Tiptoeing swiftly downstairs she watched him open the little gate at the bottom of the front garden and disappear down the bank onto the beach.

Jenny returned to her room, sat down in the dark on the edge of the bed and tried to think clearly. There was, of course, a perfectly rational explanation for Guy's furtive behavior. He had been unable to fall asleep, had decided to go for a walk on the beach and had crept out of bed to avoid waking her.

Jenny only wished she could believe it.

She clenched her fists in the darkness. All her earlier anxieties, her distress and her confusion came rushing back. It was useless to sit in the dark tormenting herself with unanswerable questions. Even a walk along a lonely beach at night was preferable to that.

Switching on the light she wriggled out of her nightdress and began to pull on her clothes.

FIVE

Anne woke up.

The moon was shining. There was a brightness around the edge of the curtains. The moon was shining, and murmuring in her ears was the distant roar of the sea.

The moonlight always looked so beautiful on the ocean. She could remember how it had looked on that other night, remember each detail of the sand and surf and cliffs.

Springing out of bed she ran to the window, drew the curtain and stared out into the night.

The tide was coming in and the sands had shrunk to a thin silver arc.

The sea was so very beautiful.

Below her window the front door closed softly and

Anne saw the girl run soundlessly down the path to the beach.

Guy's wife. Except that the red-haired girl couldn't be Guy's wife because Guy's wife was Christina. Yet the girl was Guy's wife and Guy's wife was Christina.

Anne said aloud—clearly so that They could hear— "Evil must be destroyed." Her voice sounded so odd that she laughed. Too melodramatic. She tried again, tried to sound calm and logical so that They would understand: "You see, if I don't kill her she'll kill me."

That sounded better. She thought she saw Them nod in approval. For a moment she stood listening in case They said anything, but there was no comment and the only sound she heard was the distant drone of the sea.

Fumbling in the dark she pulled on some underclothes and hunted for a pair of slacks and a sweater. She wished she could have switched on the light but They might not have liked that and anyway she had no desire to disturb Grace. Grace was so fussy, always wanting to protect her from Them; she failed to understand that sometimes Anne liked to be with Them, and often much preferred their company to the terror of loneliness. Of course, sometimes if she offended Them They could be far more terrifying than mere loneliness and then she was glad of Grace's protection, but tonight . . .

Tonight the moon was up and the night air was fresh and the sea was so very beautiful.

She tried the door which as usual Grace had locked. Anne never objected for she had long known she could escape from the room if she wanted to. The old house had low ceilings so that upstairs the distance from the window to the ground was less than it might have been in a modern house, and there was such a useful drainpipe running down the side of the house from the eaves. . . .

Anne had been the star of her school gym class. Shinning down a drainpipe was to her as easy as turning a somersault.

In the garden seconds later she wiped her hands meticulously on the seat of her slacks and stood listening for a moment.

They were there. She couldn't see Them, but she heard Them whispering and she knew They would guide her. With silent precision she left the garden, scrambled down the bank and carefully began to follow Jenny's footsteps across the shining sands.

6

ONE

Guy was a long way ahead of Jenny, and although she thought she could see him in the distance, the Downs at the head of the beach cast odd shadows so that it was hard for her to be certain. She followed his footprints to the path up the cliffs at the far end of the bay, and began the long zigzagging climb to Cellanporth. There were no more footprints now for the path was stony, and by the time she reached the garden wall at the back of the pub and hauled herself up to the street she was wondering how she would guess which way Guy had gone. There was no sign of him. Peering toward the church she saw that the street was deserted and that most of the cottages were already in darkness. There were lights on in the pub, however, and the faint sound of a wireless drifted through an open window in the kitchen. She had just stepped out into the road when she noticed the car which was partially hidden by the stone wall flanking the parking field.

But there was no mistaking the roof or windows. They belonged to the St. Cellans' Rolls Royce.

Jenny stood staring at it. Nothing happened. At last she nerved herself to cross the road, walk through the gateway into the field and peer through the windows.

The car was empty.

She had just stepped back into the road in front of the pub when she glanced out to the headland and saw something move beyond the white humps of sleeping sheep. She held her breath. The movement flickered again, two shadows dark against the moonlit landscape, and although they were too far away for her to be able to identify them she knew instinctively that one of those shadows belonged to Guy.

The stone wall bordering the field stretched out for several yards. Keeping close to it Jenny passed the warning notice and moved quickly down the track which led along the cliffs to the Snake's Tail. Deciding that she needed better cover Jenny scrambled over the bordering wall and crept across another field. It was only then that she summoned the courage to look at the two figures now only a few yards away from her across the headland.

A sheep bleated, making her jump. Crouching on the

ground she put her fingers along the uneven top of the
wall and raised her head.

They were nearer than she had realized. The wind,
blowing away from her, made it impossible to hear what
they were saying, but she was still close enough to see
them clearly. Sharply silhouetted in the moonlight, Emma
St. Cellan stood earnestly talking to Guy.

TWO

Anne reached the pub and stepped out into the road. Everywhere was silent and still. The Rolls was there, but
then it had been that other night when Charles had driven
her and Christina and some other people from Trecellan
Hall to the headland after the party. That was about the
last thing she could recall and even that scene seemed
blurred, although she could remember saying she was
hungry and someone giving her a sugar cube. She hadn't
eaten much at the party because she had been dieting, but
that had been a mistake because there it was, late at
night, and she had been starving.

And here it was, late at night again, and in front of her
was the Rolls Royce. But where was Christina? Anne
looked around swiftly. She was standing in the field beside
the car, and as she glanced toward the headland she saw
far away at the end of the next field the girl crouching behind the wall. There were two other people beyond the
sheep, but that wasn't surprising because a lot of the
guests had come out here from Trecellan Hall with them.

Anne thought quickly. If she could creep up on
Christina . . .

A hand brushed her cheek. Hard fingers sealed her lips

to muffle her gasp of terror. Her last coherent thought before panic took possession of her mind was: It's not Christina. It's someone else.

THREE

Jenny was running. She was running along the beach back to the distant white speck of the Rectory, her breath coming in great gasps which hurt her lungs and tore at her throat. Tears made it hard for her to see where she was going, but there was nothing before her except the sand, and although she stumbled twice she did not fall. In front of the Rectory she paused to regain her self control and the sea roared soothingly in her ears as she fumbled for a handkerchief.

She couldn't blot earlier scenes from her mind, Emma saying, "You knew, of course, that I was Guy's mistress," Guy insisting, "Emma means nothing to me, Jenny," and later, much later, Guy murmuring innocently, "I think I'll have an early night . . ."

She was starting to cry again. Making a determined effort she dashed away her tears and scrambled up the bank toward the gate.

The front door was on the latch just as she had left it. Slipping into the hall she closed the door behind her, tiptoed upstairs and undressed once more, putting on her nightdress.

After rearranging the pillows on her side of the bed she slipped between the sheets, forced herself to stop thinking and resolutely returned to the problems of Anna Karenina.

Two minutes later she put the book aside, turned out

the light and lay waiting in the darkness. It was impossible to read—impossible to do anything except wait for Guy to come back and wonder again and again why he had chosen to have a secret rendezvous with Emma St. Cellan.

She waited for a long time. The luminous dial of her clock glowed in the darkness, and soon the hands had crawled past midnight. It was at half-past twelve, just as Jenny had decided that she could not bear to wait for a second longer, that she heard the back door close, and leaping out of bed she ran from the room and hurried downstairs.

The door of the kitchen opened; she was about to exclaim "Guy!" in relief, when she saw that she was facing not Guy at all but Ted.

"Oh, it's *you!*" she said before she could stop herself. Pride instinctively made her avoid all mention of Guy and his exploits, so to stop Ted from saying surprised, "Who else could it have been?" she said in a rush, "I couldn't think who it was—I was on my way downstairs to get a drink of water—I didn't know you worked so late at the pub."

"I don't usually." Ted sounded glum. His eyes were tired and there was a drawn look about his mouth. "I must have been crazy. Dad went out soon after closing time and I decided to switch on the TV to keep me company while I finished the washing up. There was a film on. Ingrid Bergman. I didn't mean to get involved but before I knew where I was THE END was flashing on the screen and it was after midnight. I don't know what the time is now but I feel as if it's about four in the morning."

"I like Ingrid Bergman too." She suddenly wondered if

Leonard, leaving the pub not long after ten-thirty, had seen Guy with Emma. "Why did your father go out?" she said impulsively. "Wouldn't it have been a bit late for making visits?"

"He has a lady friend in Porthmawgan." Ted sounded even more glum. "Well, if you'll excuse me, I think I'll go up to bed."

"Yes, of course—I'm sorry if I've been keeping you up." Jenny spoke rapidly to cover her embarrassment that she had pried details of Leonard's private life from his son.

Someone was awake upstairs. They could hear footsteps, and as Ted moved to the foot of the stairs Grace called sharply from the landing, "Ted, is that Anne downstairs with you?"

"Anne! No, it's Jenny." He stared up at her. "Why? Isn't Anne in her room?"

"No, I've just looked. She's gone." Grace was running downstairs as she spoke. "The window was open and I think she must have escaped by climbing down the drainpipe—I'd never even noticed the wretched thing before. Well, there's no sense in crying over spilled milk. She's gone and now we've got to find her." She hurried past them into the living room. "I'm going to phone Roger. Jenny, perhaps you could tell Guy."

"Yes, of course," said Jenny, and realized with fright that she had locked herself into acting a part she had no wish to play. Damn Guy, she thought fiercely and turned aside to hide her tears. Damn him.

"How did you find out she was gone, Grace?" Ted was saying shaken. "What made you get up and look in her room?"

"Something woke me—I suppose you coming in. But

when I saw the time I thought it was too late for it to be you. So just to be on the safe side I thought I'd check on Anne. Her door was still locked, but as soon as I went in I saw the open window and I knew she'd gone even before I saw the empty bed." She was dialing Roger's number. "I should have guessed there was going to be trouble. She hasn't been herself all day, thanks to Charles and Emma St. Cellan."

Another door opened upstairs.

"What on earth's going on?" called Marguerite. "Why is everyone up? What's happened?"

"Anne's gone," said Ted abruptly. "Grace is phoning Roger."

"Gone!" Marguerite paused halfway down the stairs. "Gone where?"

"Just gone. Look, Mother, why don't you go back to bed and try to get some rest? We'll handle this."

"How sweet of you, darling, but of course I can't possibly do that. What a ghastly crisis! I'll get dressed straight away."

In the living room Grace had left the phone. "I'm going to take my car along the road between Cellanporth and Porthmawgan on the other side of the Downs," she said, returning to the hall. "Roger's going to take the road which goes the other way to Meryon's Landing. Perhaps you could drive a few miles along the road to Castlesea, Mrs. Stratton, and that would leave Guy and Ted free to search the beach."

"I'll walk along the beach toward Cellanporth," Ted said at once. He turned to Jenny. "Tell Guy to go toward Porthmawgan."

"Yes," said Jenny automatically. "All right."

"Supposing Anne manages to elude us all," said Marguerite, "and comes back to the house?"

"That's a thought," said Grace. "Perhaps Guy had better stay here with Jenny. I don't think she should tackle Anne on her own."

Panic gripped Jenny so violently that she felt physically ill. All the events of that evening, the tension of following Guy to Cellanporth, the shock of discovering him with Emma and now the fear of knowing she would be alone in the house while Anne roamed somewhere outside—all combined to make her dizzy with nausea. She just managed to reach the cloakroom before she was sick, and afterwards she felt so shaken that she had to sit down on one of the chairs in the kitchen.

The front door slammed as Ted went down to the beach. Presently Grace, fully dressed this time, ran through the kitchen on her way to the garage.

"Good heavens!" she exclaimed as Jenny rose guiltily from her chair. "Are you still down here?"

"I . . . felt dizzy for a moment and had to sit down."

"Are you all right now?"

"Yes. Fine. I'll go upstairs."

"Yes, for God's sake wake Guy and tell him what's going on," said Grace, and disappeared into the courtyard.

Jenny hurried upstairs and subsided weakly onto the bed in her empty room. She had been sitting there for about five minutes when the door of Marguerite's bedroom opened and Marguerite's footsteps crossed the landing to the stairs. Jenny waited, listening. After the sound of the Cortina's engine had faded into the distance, she got up and went to the door to lock it.

There was no key.

In panic she ran downstairs, bolted the back door and put the front door on its chain. After that she felt less frightened but the dizzyness was returning and in desperation she began to search for some brandy. There was a bottle in the cupboard under the dining room sideboard. She was just helping herself to a stiff measure when she heard the movement outside the front door, the faint scratching at the lock, and the glass of brandy slipped through her fingers to shatter on the polished boards of the floor.

For three seconds she stood stock still, unable to breathe, and then very slowly she went to the window and moved the edge of the curtain.

Clouds now blotted out the moonlight. The front garden was full of shadows, but there was still enough light for Jenny to see that the figure struggling quietly with the front door was Guy, not Anne.

Sobbing with relief she ran into the hall to let him in.

"Jenny! Darling, what's the matter? Why are you up? Why are all the lights on?"

The enormity of relief was swept away by the rising tide of her anger. She looked up at him fiercely. "Where were you?"

"I walked to Cellanporth. Jenny, what *is* the matter? What's been happening?"

"Why did you have to go to Cellanporth?"

He glanced swiftly up the stairs. "Shhh! You'll wake everyone."

"No one's here."

"What!"

"They're all looking for Anne. She's run away."

He stared at her in shocked silence.

"Guy, why did you go to Cellanporth?"

"When was Anne discovered missing? How long has everyone been gone?"

As if to mark the impasse in their conversation the telephone shrilled in the living room. Jenny followed him to the doorway and watched him as he picked up the receiver.

"Hullo?" she heard him say flatly, and then the next moment he was exclaiming in an incredulous voice: "What? . . . When? All right, never mind. I'll be over straight away. No—wait! Marguerite and Grace are both out looking for her so both cars are gone. You'll have to bring her here yourself. I'm sorry." He replaced the receiver and turned once more to Jenny.

"That was Charles St. Cellan," he said slowly at last. "He says Anne is with him at Trecellan Hall."

FOUR

"But my dear Guy," drawled Charles, "I found her wandering around by my Rolls Royce which was parked in the field opposite the pub! What else could I have done but capture her—in the nicest possible way, naturally. I mean, I had to do something. I didn't want to leave her wandering around the cliffs at some godforsaken hour of the night, so I though the best thing for me to do was to take her back to the Hall."

"Why didn't you bring her straight back to the Rectory?"

"I . . ." Charles decided this question was too difficult to answer and made an effort to slip around it. "I tried to phone you but the line was engaged. So I waited, tried to talk to Anne, soothe her, calm her down—you know, all that sort of thing—even made her some tea. For God's sake, Guy, you surely don't think I raped her, do you? I was only trying to help."

"I want to know why you took Anne to the Hall instead of bringing her straight home to the Rectory."

Charles cast around in his mind for inspiration. "I thought there must have been some reason why she ran away, and I didn't like to take her to the Rectory until I knew you'd got back."

"Back from where?" Marguerite interrupted in surprise.

"I don't believe one word you say," said Guy to Charles. "Not one word."

"For Christ's sake, Guy, I'd have thought you'd be grateful to me for rescuing your sister!"

"Look, Charles. You brought Anne back here in a bad state. Roger's had to give her all kinds of sedatives to calm her down. I think the least I'm entitled to do in the circumstances is to ask you a question or two."

"Well, if it comes to that, I could ask *you* a question or two! Where's my sister?"

"We're discussing my sister, not yours." Jenny saw Guy's fists clench and realized that he was on the verge of losing his temper. She glanced around in despair. Marguerite sat on the sofa as she nursed the dregs of her cup of coffee and listened to the conversation with a curiosity she made no effort to conceal. Guy and Charles stood facing each other upon the hearth, and beyond them on the mantel shelf the hands of the French clock pointed to quarter to two. Upstairs all was quiet. Roger Carpenter had departed; Grace was alone with Anne, and Ted was already asleep in his room.

"Well, you boys are obviously going to wrangle till

dawn," said Marguerite, standing up at last and smoothing her hands over her skirt as if to suppress her impatience. "Personally I think you're both being just the tiniest bit silly. After all, Anne's back, isn't she? That's the main thing. Perhaps Charles should have brought her straight back to the Rectory instead of taking her to the Hall, but he brought her back in the end and that's what matters. Why don't you both call it a day and then we can all go and get some sleep?"

Guy ignored her. "What were you doing at the pub at that time of night anyway, Charles?"

"Just gossiping with Leonard after hours—is that a crime? I was waiting for Emma, as if you hadn't already guessed. Finally I got tired of waiting and went outside to see if she was coming and that's when I bumped into Anne. I decided that I'd better get Anne away and thought that when Emma arrived she could wait at the pub till I came back."

"Then why did you ask me where Emma was? She's obviously still waiting there faithfully."

"But she's not! I made a slight detour on my way here just now and stopped at the pub to pick her up, but Leonard didn't answer the doorbell and there was no sign of Emma at all. What did you do with her?"

"What do you mean?"

"You had a rendezvous with her, didn't you?"

"I've better things to do with my time."

"Really, Charles," said Marguerite, "why on earth should you think that Guy—who's practically on his honeymoon—would have a midnight rendezvous with your sister? She must have just got tired of waiting for you at the pub and decided to walk back to the Hall. You'll probably find her there when you get back—whenever that may be."

Charles was beginning to look confused. Marguerite's hint that he should leave made no impression on him. "But of course you met Emma!" he said angrily to Guy. "You must have done!"

"Did you see me with her?"

"No, I was in the pub. But—"

"Then your only reason for saying that Emma met me tonight is that Emma herself said she intended to do so."

"But—"

"Look, Charles, we're all very tired. We all want to go to bed. Why don't you go home? Emma's probably there waiting for you by this time. I'm grateful to you for bringing Anne back and I'm sorry I've been short-tempered with you, but I'm sure you realize that I've been under considerable strain."

Charles shrugged and moved towards the door. "All right, what does it matter? I'll find out the truth soon enough. I might have known you wouldn't admit to anything in front of your wife and stepmother."

"What an extraordinary young man he is," said Marguerite after he left. "But the St. Cellans have always had the reputation for being an odd family . . . well, I'm off to bed. Sleep well, both of you."

They each murmured "goodnight" and waited till she had closed the door. "She obviously didn't know I was out tonight," said Guy at last in a low voice. "Are you the only one who knows?"

Jenny managed to nod.

"Thank God for that. After all the fuss Charles made

no one would ever believe me if I said I went for a walk along the beach because I couldn't sleep."

Jenny tried to speak again but couldn't and he turned toward the door saying, "Shall we go to bed? I'm very tired and if I don't get to bed soon I'll go to sleep standing up." After that there seemed nothing to do except follow him upstairs to their room. When she arrived he was already peeling off his clothes, and by the time she had nerved herself to reopen the conversation he had fallen asleep.

FIVE

Jenny lay awake for a long time in the dark. Two of Guy's comments tormented her. The first had been made after the phone call from Charles; Jenny had asked Guy a third time why he had gone to Cellanporth and he had evaded her question yet again by saying with more than a hint of irritation: "Darling, I know you're cross because I went for a midnight stroll without you, but would you really have been pleased if I'd woken you up to say I couldn't sleep and was going out?" When she had remained silent he had gone into the kitchen to make coffee and a sandwich. Charles had arrived before Guy had come back to the living room and soon after that the others had begun to straggle back to the rectory.

The other comment which Jenny now recalled in such painful detail was Guy saying to her, "No one would ever believe me if I said I went for a walk along the beach because I couldn't sleep." Twice Guy had implied that insomnia had been responsible for his stealthy departure from the house, but on neither occasion had he said positively, "Look, this is what I did. I went for a walk along the beach. I went because I couldn't sleep." He had somehow managed, she saw now, to avoid an outright lie.

But an outright lie might almost have been preferable to such evasiveness.

She saw too that it would be very difficult for her to say next morning, "I know you met Emma last night," because this would underline his evasions and make him look not only deceitful but a fool. The moment for disclosing her knowledge had come and gone; she realized now that by staying silent she had maneuvered herself into a position where to say nothing was hard but to say what she wanted to say was downright dangerous.

When she woke at dawn after a brief doze she knew she could never get back to sleep, so taking great care not to disturb Guy she slipped out of bed, pulled on her clothes and went outside.

The pale sky was streaked with pink and gold as the sun rose behind the Downs and far away across the sands the tide was on the turn. Jenny scrambled down to the beach. There was no one in sight. As she paused to look about her she saw only the wheeling gulls and, far away on the headland, the white dots of the sheep motionless near the edge of the cliffs. She began to walk toward the headland, and the wind tugged at her hair until it streamed behind her like a ragged banner.

She walked and walked and walked.

After a while she realized she was talking to herself. She only thought aloud when she was profoundly unhappy, but it soothed her. She loved Guy, she kept saying. She couldn't bear to quarrel with him, couldn't bear it if things went wrong, couldn't bear him lying to her about Emma St. Cellan . . .

Why *had* Guy met Emma anyway?

She looked in despair at the cliffs ahead of her. Below them on the sand lay something white and still, but after the first shock had sent the blood rushing from her face she remembered what Ted had told her about the sheep. The huddled shape on the beach ahead of her was no reincarnation of Christina but merely the corpse of an unfortunate animal who had wandered too close to the edge.

Yet it was amazing how human the body looked. It was, of course, an optical illusion created by distance, but. . . .

She suddenly realized that there was no optical illusion.

She tried to stop then, but her feet carried her forward. She wanted to scream but something had happened to her chest so that even breathing was almost impossible. She simply went on walking, drawn to the corpse by a terrible fascination, and soon she realized that the dull white which she had mistaken for sheep's wool was instead a pair of sodden slacks, while the sand-streaked black which she had assumed was a small rock was in reality a sweater clinging to a mangled body. A mass of wet dull hair hid the entire front of the head, and Jenny was glad because she knew she would have fainted if she had seen Emma's face.

She was thinking aloud again in a voice which she did not recognize because it sounded so calm. The voice said that since the face was hidden everything was quite all right. It was impossible to faint because the face was hidden. There was no possibility whatsoever of her fainting because she could not faint if she did not see the face.

A gust of wind stirred the wet hair and revealed the ravaged face beneath.

Jenny screamed.

And then suddenly there was a roaring in her ears, and the sand, hard and wet, rose up from the ground to crush her.

7

ONE

"Jenny."

Someone was bending over her. Opening her eyes she saw a tilted, blurred world containing only sky and Guy's face inches from her own. He was kneeling beside her and she felt him slip his arms around her and raise her to a sitting position.

"Is that better?"

"Hm . . . " She managed to nod. "Did I pass out for long?"

"A couple of minutes."

"How did you get here so quickly?"

"I heard you leave the house and came after you. If you'd looked back you would have seen me." He paused before adding, "I wanted to talk to you about last night."

Memory grated through her consciousness. Before she

could stop herself she was swiveling around to face the corpse on the sand. "Guy—"

"Yes, I know. We'll have to get the police." He laid his hand against her cheek and turned her face gently away from Emma's sodden body.

"But Guy, what will the police think? If they knew you met Emma last night—" She stopped, but the words were already spoken and all she could do was stare at Guy's taut face.

"So you did know," he said. "I thought you did. But how the hell did you find out?"

"I woke up when you left the house and I—I followed you. I shouldn't have done—I don't know why I did—but I followed you up onto the headland and saw you with Emma—"

"My poor Jenny."

"—and I didn't know what to think—I couldn't imagine one single reason why you should have done such a thing—"

"Oh God, I'm sorry—"

"—and later when you evaded my questions—I was going to ask you about it outright but I left it too long and just didn't have the nerve—"

"Poor Jenny, I should have told you, shouldn't I? I shouldn't have kept you in the dark like that, but you see I had this horror of involving you with the St. Cellans or Anne's troubles or anything related to Christina's death, and I thought that if I could meet Emma without you knowing about it—"

"But Guy, why *did* you meet her?"

"She said she had definite proof that Anne was responsible for Christina's death and she wanted to discuss it with me. She phoned yesterday afternoon—it was that mysterious call that Grace took; Emma disguised her voice. When she called back and told me what she wanted I tried to persuade her to talk about it on the phone, but she wouldn't. She invited me to Trecellan Hall but I wasn't having that—they have a housekeeper there and I didn't want to start any rumors. And I certainly wasn't going to invite her to the Rectory. In the end I suggested we meet on the headland at eleven o'clock. I didn't want to but I was afraid she really did know something about Anne—afraid there was something Anne said yesterday in Emma's presence that Ted failed to hear . . . I felt I had to know one way or the other what it was."

"So you suggested an early night . . . " Jenny's voice trailed away.

"Yes, I wanted to be able to say to you shortly before half-past ten that I couldn't sleep and was going for a walk along the beach. If I'd waited and told you I was going for a walk before we went to bed you might have wanted to come. But I thought if you were already in bed . . ."

"Oh," said Jenny.

"In fact you were asleep soon after ten so I didn't have to say anything. I was nearly asleep myself—the last thing I wanted to do was crawl out of bed and trudge off to Cellanporth! I shouldn't have made love to you earlier but you were so irresistible that I couldn't help myself."

"Oh!" said Jenny, and managed to return his smile. The relief of learning that his passion had been spontaneous took an enormous weight off her mind. She began to feel better.

"Anyway," Guy was saying, "I dragged myself over to Cellanporth, met Emma and discovered that I'd been wasting my time. She hadn't proof at all. After an enormous amount of unnecessary talk she finally asked me why Anne had called Charles a murderer, and by that time I was so furious that I refused to answer."

Jenny was baffled. "Was that really her only reason for seeing you?"

"No, of course it wasn't," Guy said wryly. "She had a bet with her wretched brother that she'd be able to lure me to a secret rendezvous even though I had remarried. She used Anne as a bait. That was all."

"What did you say when you found out?" asked Jenny.

"Nothing. I was speechless. Then she asked me to be a good sport about it and walk back to the pub to show Charles who'd won the bet. I told her to go to hell and set off without her. She made no effort to catch me up; just laughed and followed at her own pace—she was still some yards behind me when I reached the road and took the footpath down to the beach." He paused. "That was the last I saw of her."

It never occurred to Jenny to disbelieve him. She was busy fighting the terrible urge to look behind them again at Emma's body. "How lucky Charles didn't walk out of the pub and see you," she said.

"By then he must have taken Anne off to the Hall," Guy answered. "I was thinking about that, trying to remember if the Rolls was still opposite the pub, and I'm almost sure it was gone."

Jenny made a great effort to concentrate. "I think it had left even before I went back. I didn't specially notice at the time, but now I'm almost certain that the field was empty then. Guy." She broke off. A small core of doubt nagged unpleasantly at the back of her mind.

"Yes?"

"I ran away while you were still talking to Emma, but surely she couldn't have kept you for over an hour after that? Why was it so long before you reached the Rectory?"

"Well, you'll never believe it after all my evasions and double-talk," said Guy ruefully, "but I really did go for a walk. I was disturbed by the meeting with Emma and thinking so hard about Anne and Christina that when I reached the Rectory I knew I'd never be able to sleep. I left the beach, but didn't go into the house. I walked over the Downs until I reached the spot where you can look down on Trecellan Hall, and then I turned and came back. You can imagine what a shock it was when I saw all the lights were on at the Rectory. I was sure my absence must have been discovered."

"But no one knows you were missing," said Jenny slowly, "and no one knows you met Emma. Except me."

"And no one knows you followed me and saw us together." Guy grimaced. "All anyone knows is that Emma went out onto the headland to meet me and about ten minutes later Anne was found wandering outside the pub. Charles will testify to that."

"You don't mean—"

"Yes, I do. Anne's the perfect scapegoat." He dug his heel sharply into the sand and stared at the deep mark. "Everything will be all right," he said slowly, "if Emma went back into the pub after I left her. As long as Leonard or Ted saw her after Charles picked up Anne, no one will think Anne responsible."

"Supposing Emma told them she'd met you!" said Jenny in sudden panic.

"I'd say she was trying to save face," he said without hesitation, and it occurred to her uneasily how glib he could be. "Jenny, I'm going to brazen it out and say I never met Emma. We must both insist that we never left the Rectory last night."

"But Guy——" Her uneasiness was deepening with every word he spoke.

"Darling, it must be—has to be—the only thing to do, can't you see? What do you suppose the police will think if they know I had a secret meeting with Emma—and that you found out about it? They'd find it all too easy to assign a motive to each of us."

"But if they don't suspect us they'll suspect Anne!" cried Jenny, very upset by this time. "And we're the only ones who know that when Anne went off to Trecellan Hall with Charles, Emma was still alive. If we say we were both at the Rectory there'll be no proof that Anne's innocent!"

"But I think either Leonard or Ted will be able to prove Emma was alive after Anne left with Charles. And even if they can't—even if Emma never went back into the pub——" he drew a deep breath "—I could still give Anne some sort of alibi. If I say I never left the Rectory I could also say that I spoke to Anne only half an hour before Charles met her in Cellanporth. That would make it impossible for her to have killed Emma. It's a twenty-five minute walk from the Rectory just to the pub."

"But you don't know what time Charles met Anne!" Jenny felt close to despair. "You've no idea what time it was!"

"Yes, I have," Guy said calmly. "Charles said it was about ten past eleven and that sounds right: I met Emma at eleven and by ten past you would have been out on the headland too. You didn't stay long but by the time you went back past the pub the Rolls was already gone . . ." He drew her closer to him and slipped his arm around her waist again. "It'll be all right, darling, I promise. It'll be all right." And after a moment he added gently, "You've had a bad shock. Later on when you're better things won't seem so difficult."

Jenny said rapidly, "If only it could have been an accident! If only the autopsy would reveal traces of drugs—"

"They'll never believe it could happen twice," said Guy. "Christina's death—yes. There were a dozen witnesses to back up the autopsy findings. But Emma? Emma, unfortunately, was stone-cold sober. I don't think an autopsy is going to help matters at all."

"But Guy, who could have killed her?"

"Some stray lunatic of a holiday maker, I should think, with rape in mind. Emma probably went over the cliff as the result of a struggle." He paused before adding uneasily, "The police will catch him all the sooner if we don't complicate matters by making ourselves suspects."

"I suppose so . . . yes." Jenny shivered as she thought of Emma struggling for her life.

The long silence which followed was broken only when Guy asked anxiously, "How are you feeling now? Do you think you're well enough to walk back to the Rectory?"

"I think so, yes." Her legs still felt unsteady but the fresh sea breeze cleared her head so that she felt stronger. "Yes, I'm all right," she said shakily. "Let's go."

The sun shone from cloudless skies as they walked back to the Rectory, and far away in the distance across the deserted beach the sand dunes of Porthmawgan gleamed like white gold.

At last Guy said, "Darling, do you really think I'm wrong not to tell the police the whole story? I'm convinced that it would do more harm than good, but if you really feel we ought to tell the truth—"

"No, let's do as you say." She was thinking not of herself, but of the police suspecting Guy, arresting him and taking him away from her. Anything would be better than that, and it would be so easy to say to the police that she had never left the Rectory . . . "I think you're right," she said strongly. "I know you're right." But her conscience stirred uneasily.

TWO

"Dead!" said Marguerite as if Emma had committed some extraordinary social faux pas.

"Dead," said Guy. "On the beach. Jenny and I both saw her."

They were all in the kitchen. Bacon sizzled on the stove and nearby the percolator was bubbling quietly.

Marguerite was wearing a powder-blue peignoir, a soupçon of mascara and an expression of amazed disbelief. "Oh my God, Guy, you don't suppose . . . Guy, I've come to a decision. Anne must be in a proper home. The responsibility—well, I mean, it's just not fair to Grace—or me—although speaking for myself I don't mind . . ."

"We'll discuss it later, Marguerite," Guy said abruptly, and moved past her into the hall. "I'm going to phone the police."

"The police! You mean you think Anne—"

"I don't think anything, Marguerite. Emma's dead and the police have to be told and that's all there is to say."

"But if the police start to make inquiries—they'll find out Anne was missing last night—"

"Marguerite, I'm not discussing this with you at present. I'm sorry . . . hullo, is this the police? This is Guy

Stratton of the Rectory-by-the-Sea. I want to report a death . . ."

THREE

"Good heavens," said Grace. Coming downstairs to collect breakfast trays for Anne and herself she heard Guy on the phone. "Was it an accident?"

"My dear," said Marguerite, "even if it was, do you suppose the police will believe it once they hear about Anne?"

"I've no idea," said Grace, "but I can't imagine why poor Anne should want to launch a homicidal attack on Emma St. Cellan."

"But Grace, Anne isn't responsible for her actions!"

"To some extent, no," agreed Grace, "but to some extent, yes. She's actually very logical and I can't think of a single reason why she should want to kill Emma."

Ted said from the top of the stairs, "What's going on? What's happened?" He wore a pair of old-fashioned striped pajamas, and his tousled fair hair was standing on end. "You woke me up," he added accusingly.

"Darling, the most extraordinary and dreadful thing has happened," said Marguerite. "Emma St. Cellan is dead—just like Christina. Guy and Jenny found her on the beach this morning and Guy's just phoning the police."

Guy came out of the living room and glanced up. "Ted, did you see Emma last night after Charles had left the pub? Did she come back into the pub to look for him?"

There was a silence. Ted still looked blank. When he

managed to speak all he said was an incredulous, "Dead? Emma?"

"Yes, and I doubt if it was an accident. I've just spoken to P.C. Thomas and he's going to get in touch with the higher powers at Castlesea. What was the name of that detective-inspector who made the inquiries into Christina's death?"

"Davies," said Marguerite promptly. "A quiet, pleasant man, very tactful for a policeman. Detective-Inspector Davies, and his assistant was Detective-Sergeant—now what was the sergeant's name? Something Welsh. Ah yes, Rhys. That was it. We were lucky to have two such nice men handling that appalling business."

"Let's hope we'll be as lucky this time. At any rate it seems likely that one of the first things the police will try to establish is who was the last to see Emma. Now, Charles said last night that he was expecting her to come back to the pub—"

"She didn't come back," said Ted. He thought for a moment before adding, "Or if she did, I didn't see her. I was at the back of the house in the kitchen—washing glasses and watching TV."

"Was Leonard there?"

"No, he went off a couple of minutes after Charles left. It was about a quarter past eleven by then. I noticed because I took off my watch before starting the glasses. I didn't want it to get wet."

"And where," said Marguerite, "was Leonard going at quarter past eleven at night?"

"Perhaps you'd like to ask him yourself," said Ted very politely and disappeared in the direction of the bathroom.

"Guy," said Grace before the pause became awkward,

"I'd like to phone Roger. I think he should know about this."

"I'll do it," said Guy briefly and vanished into the living room again.

"Well, I must say," said Marguerite, "it's all very odd. Of course Emma *was* wild. I expect there was some man involved—no doubt I'm leaping to the wrong conclusion about poor Anne. Oh dear! Why did she have to pick last night to go on an escapade?"

"I'd better take Anne's breakfast up to her," said Grace, "I want her routine to remain as calm as usual. Excuse me, please." Marguerite followed her to the kitchen, and when Guy finished talking to Roger, Jenny was alone. "Ted didn't see her," he said in a low voice.

"No. Perhaps Leonard—although if he left very soon after Charles—"

"It's worth trying," said Guy, and began to dial the St. Cellan Arms.

FOUR

"Wait a minute," said Leonard. "You have to be joking."

"No, it's true, I'm afraid. Leonard, you didn't see her, did you, after Charles left?"

"Hold it," said Leonard. "Hold everything." He put down the receiver, went to the bar, poured himself a shot of brandy and drank it before picking up the receiver again. "Guy? No, I didn't see her. She and Charles stayed after closing time the way they do sometimes, and I was watching the clock because I had a date with a certain lady friend and Emma was watching the clock because she had a date with a certain gentleman friend—all very secret, you know how it is. So out she goes at ten to eleven, all mysterious and romantic, and Charles and I sit around nattering some more for about twenty minutes. Finally I say to Charles, 'Look, I have to be going now if you don't mind, mate, because Emma's not the only one tonight with a bloody assignation.' So he says, 'Okay, don't get shirty, I'll just see if Emma's coming back.' So he goes outside and that's the last I see of him—when I leave about two minutes later his car's gone and naturally I think he met Emma and they went off home together. Okay? So off I go, happy as a lark, down the street to the garage which I rent for my car, and that's that. But I didn't see Emma again. Look, she must have joined up with Charles the moment he left, surely? Why else would he go home and leave her stranded?"

"He expected she could stay at the pub till he was able to pick her up later. He'd found my sister wandering around outside the pub and for some reason best known to himself he took her back to Trecellan Hall for a while."

"For Christ's sake! Was Anne all right?"

"Well, she hasn't spoken a word to anyone since she got back and I'm expecting Roger at any moment . . ."

Five minutes later the doctor's car was in the courtyard. Guy opened the back door to greet him. "Come upstairs, Roger. Thanks for coming so quickly."

Gripping the handle of his doctor's bag very tightly Roger said, "How is she this morning?"

"Much the same as when you saw her last night. She still hasn't said a word."

Roger was very white. "You've reported Emma's death, of course. I suppose the police surgeon will deal with the autopsy . . . God, what a ghastly thing." He broke off. "Was Emma alive after Charles picked up Anne?"

"Nobody seems to know the answer to that, but it's impossible that Anne was involved. I saw her in her room only half an hour before Charles found her in Cellanporth. She wouldn't have had time for an encounter with Emma."

"You're sure about the time?"

"Positive."

Roger's shoulders slumped a little in relief. "I can't imagine why on earth she would try to kill Emma, but I suppose if she was hallucinating and thought Emma was Christina—"

"I know."

"Even so I don't believe Anne would have attacked her. I would never have let Anne leave the nursing home if I'd thought she was dangerous—"

"I know, Roger. Don't worry about it. If the police do suspect Anne at least I'm in a position to prove to them that their suspicions are groundless."

"I see." Their glances met for a long moment before Roger added without inflection, "I hope the police believe you."

"Don't you believe me?"

"I want to. That's all that matters." He walked to the stairs. "I'd better see her straight away. If the police are already on their way here every second counts."

Grace emerged from Anne's sitting room as Guy followed Roger to the floor above.

"She won't eat," she said in a low voice, "and she won't talk."

Roger nodded. They went into the sitting-room and Guy closed the door behind him.

"Hullo, Anne," said Roger calmly, setting down his bag. "I hear you went for a walk last night."

She smiled at him, a small secret smile, but said nothing.

"Why did you feel like going for a walk?"

She did not answer but stared dreamily out of the window at the sea.

"It was a lovely night, wasn't it," said Roger, sitting down on the window seat beside her. "I was out looking for you for a while in case you'd got lost, and I thought at the time how beautiful the countryside was in the moonlight."

Anne traced a pattern idly on the windowpane and smiled again.

"Did you meet anyone when you were out, Anne?"

She shook her head.

"No one at all?"

She shook her head again.

"What about Charles St. Cellan? You met him, didn't you?"

She looked thoughtful, then cunning. Presently she shook her head a third time.

"I thought you met Charles."

There was a pause. Anne stared at the windowsill but at last said, "That part wasn't real."

"Not real?"

"No."

"Why wasn't it real?"

"It didn't count." She smiled again at her hands. "You see, I knew I had to kill her because she was going to kill me. But I lost her. I think she must have gone over the cliff. Like Christina. But it didn't matter because Charles was there to protect me and he wouldn't have let her kill me, would he? At least I thought it was Charles, but actually it was someone else. I wish I had contact lenses. I hate to wear my glasses—they look so horrible and make me seem at least thirty. Daddy always said I could have contact lenses but Daddy died. And Christina died too—or so everyone thinks, but you see, she didn't die and now she's pretending to be someone else." She turned to Grace. "Is there any more coffee? Ask Roger if he'd like some coffee."

"Coffee, Roger?" said Grace tranquilly.

"Not at the moment, thanks. I've just remembered there's something I want to ask Ted. Excuse me for a minute, please, Anne. Guy, could you come and help me find Ted?"

They withdrew to the landing; Guy immediately led the way into his bedroom and closed the door. Outside the Downs still shimmered in the sunlight and a bird chirped beyond the window that Jenny had left open to air the room.

"Well?"

"She must go to the nursing home," said Roger. His voice was uneven, his eyes opaque. "At once. I'll make the arrangements and try to make it as difficult as possible for the police to interview her."

"You think—"

"I think what you think," said Roger, "and you'd better make damned sure the police believe you when you say you spoke to Anne less than half an hour before she met Charles in Cellanporth."

8

ONE

The sleek black police car purred along the country roads which stretched from the outskirts of Castlesea to Cellanporth. The morning was still brilliantly clear, and in the distance the Downs which bordered the sea formed a spectacular horizon.

"Lovely weather for a holiday," said Chief Detective-Inspector Davies, gazing admiringly at the cloudless skies.

"Mr. Stratton doesn't have much luck with his holidays," observed Detective-Sergeant Rhys.

"No, he doesn't, does he?" Davies was still watching the sky. "This is a rum business, Rhys. I always wondered if we ever got to the bottom of that case a year ago, and if my hunch is right this new case will prove we didn't. What do you think?"

"Well, sir, it would look that way. I mean, the two cases must be related, wouldn't you say? Same people involved, same type of death, same cliff—"

"But a different corpse. How well do you remember Miss St. Cellan, Rhys?"

"Remarkably well, sir. A very fast young lady, as my grandmother would have said. She gave Mr. Stratton his alibi the evening Mrs. Stratton went over the cliff, but that didn't mean too much, (a) because both the lady and gentleman were a bit pickled at the time and (b) because it might have been in both their best interests to give each other alibis. But because we didn't have any proof there wasn't much we could do to interfere with the coroner's verdict of accidental death."

"Well, at least this time we shouldn't have a drug party complicating the issue. I wonder what happened to Stratton's sister—you remember the sister, of course."

"Of course, sir, a very tragic business, but a red herring as far as any possible murder went."

"You think so?"

"Oh yes, sir. No motive. Of course there was the drug angle—"

"There was the drug angle. People on drugs are capable of motiveless murder."

"But Miss Stratton was such a slim little thing, sir—I find it difficult to imagine her tossing the deceased, who was a tall willowy woman, if I remember rightly, over the cliff while under the influence. It's much easier to imagine Mr. Stratton giving his wife a good shove. Plenty of motive too, wasn't there? Money troubles and infidelity. Not at all a happy situation, I'd say."

"I'd say so too, Rhys. But why does Stratton feel the need to dispose of Miss St. Cellan nearly a year later?"

"That's easy, sir. He says to Miss St. Cellan: 'Give me an alibi for the night in question and after a year when all the fuss has died down we'll get married and live happily ever after.' But, a year passes and he has second thoughts. The lady feels put out by his dilly-dallying and threatens to tell the police all she knows unless he hurries up with the wedding ring. Stratton is then obliged to do the necessaries."

"A very intriguing theory, Rhys."

"Thank you, sir."

"It becomes all the more intriguing when you consider the fact that Stratton's just remarried."

"Has he indeed! Fancy!" Rhys thought for a moment. "Well, that might have put him in even more difficulty with Miss St. Cellan, mightn't it, sir?"

"It certainly might, Rhys." Davies gazed vaguely at a flock of sheep and rubbed his nose with the back of his hand. "It certainly might."

TWO

The long sunlit morning gave way to a clouded afternoon, and as the clock in the Rectory living room struck three the rain began to beat against the windows which faced the sea. From his position by the fireplace Davies glanced at the gray skies over the beach before saying tranquilly, "Now let me make sure I've got this right. Mr. and Mrs. Stratton went to bed soon after eight o'clock. Mrs. Stratton—that's to say, Mrs. Marguerite Stratton—" he smiled courteously at Marguerite "—sat downstairs for a while before going up to her room; following her usual habits she was in bed by ten. By that time Miss Anne Stratton was also in bed and you, Miss Reid—" he turned to Grace "—were in your room and preparing for bed."

Grace nodded.

"The only other member of the household, Mr. Ted Matthews, was in Cellanporth at the pub." Davies paused, glanced around and saw his audience was regarding him expectantly. "Now, at approximately twenty minutes to eleven, you, Mr. Stratton, got up to go to the bathroom, saw a light under your sister's door and looked in on her."

"Right," said Guy, and the American affirmation, slipping unexpectedly from his lips, seemed to Jenny to exacerbate the phoniness of his lie.

"However, immediately after you returned to your room your sister must have left the house because—and we've already confirmed this with Mr. St. Cellan whom we saw earlier—she was found wandering in Cellanporth about half an hour later, and it's at least a twenty-five minute walk from here to the pub, even if you go across the sands." Davies slipped his hands casually into his pockets. He did not look at Rhys who was sitting impassively with his notebook by the door, and yet it seemed to Jenny that some mysterious signal passed between them, a silent communication of two people who have long worked together in a certain way.

"Now," said Davies with a pensive glance at the ceiling, "just let me complete my picture. The next thing that happened after Miss Stratton left was that you returned to the house from Cellanporth, Mr. Matthews. You say that was at about twelve-thirty. And no one heard anything during that time? You heard nothing, Miss Reid?"

"Not a thing," said Grace, "although I did hear Ted come in. That's when I got up, looked in on Anne and found she was gone."

"Yes, I have a note of that. Meanwhile you, Mrs. Stratton, met Mr. Matthews in the hall on your way to the kitchen for a glass of water."

"Yes," said Jenny.

"Miss Reid then found Anne was missing and a search party which included Dr.—" He paused.

"Carpenter," said Rhys from the door.

"—Carpenter, was organized. Mrs. Marguerite Stratton and Miss Reid left in their cars, and Mr. Matthews went out to search the beach. Which way did you go, Mr. Matthews?"

"Toward Cellanporth," said Ted.

"But you obviously didn't find Miss St. Cellan's body beneath the cliffs."

"I didn't get as far as the cliffs. I was sure Anne wouldn't be there because the cliffs and caves terrified her —they reminded her of her experience last year."

"I remember, yes."

"So I only went a little way toward Cellanporth, and when there was no sign of her I turned and walked toward Porthmawgan."

"I see. Meanwhile you, Mr. Stratton, and your wife remained here at the Rectory. Why was that?"

"Someone had to stay at the house till Anne came back," Guy said evenly, "and naturally I couldn't leave my wife to wait there alone. Anne had expressed feelings of hostility toward Jenny and I didn't want Jenny coping with any unpleasant scenes."

"Hostility? Why would that be?"

"It's part of her illness. Dr. Carpenter could explain it better than I can."

"I see. And this search party—was it you who decided where each person should go?"

"No, I was still in bed."

"I organized the search party and called Dr. Carpenter," said Grace. "I felt that not a moment should be wasted so I'm afraid I didn't wait for Guy."

"I see," said Davies.

Guy said, "My wife and I waited here alone until Charles St. Cellan brought Anne back—that was at about a quarter past one, I suppose. Charles had some whiskey and stayed for half an hour—until everyone had returned."

"Mr. St. Cellan rang up to say your sister was with him, I think you said earlier."

"Yes, that was soon after everyone had left—about quarter to one."

"You took the call."

"Yes."

Davies shifted his weight from one foot to another, removed a hand from his pocket and thoughtfully inspected a fingernail. "Well, I'm obliged to you all for your assistance . . . I'll have to talk to you all again after the police surgeon has examined the body, but meanwhile—"

"But why?" said Marguerite nervously. "I mean, what more can we tell you? It was obviously an accident. I can't think why you should be so interested in what we all did."

"Just routine, Mrs. Stratton," said Davies soothingly. "It's nothing for you to worry about." He turned to Guy. "Mr. Stratton, I'd like a word with you alone, if you please."

There was a pause before Guy said, "Of course." And as Jenny began to feel weak with nervousness he added, "Come next door into the dining room."

The rain outside had brought cooler air from the Atlantic. Guy automatically stooped to switch on the electric fire and when he straightened his back again the sergeant had closed the door.

"Well, Mr. Stratton," said Davies politely, "I understand from Mr. St. Cellan that you had an appointment with his sister last night. I think I can understand why you felt it was necessary to conceal the fact from your family, but I hardly need tell you that it would be a mistake for you to conceal it from us. When did the two of you meet, how long were you together and just exactly what was the meeting all about?"

THREE

Half an hour later the police car reversed with difficulty in the Rectory courtyard and bumped away up the track toward Cellanporth.

Davies said to the silent bulk of his sergeant beside him, "What do you think, Rhys?"

"Well, sir, if she died between quarter to one and half-past one no one has the ghost of an alibi. They were all out searching except for Mr. and Mrs. Stratton. But Stratton could have killed her earlier if he met her at eleven. Do you suppose the autopsy will be able to pinpoint the exact time of death?"

"I doubt it, but regardless of the autopsy it would seem that Miss St. Cellan must have been killed much earlier than quarter to one. Otherwise why didn't she go back to the pub to look for her brother?"

"Well, if Mr. Stratton kept her talking a long time anything's possible, I suppose, sir."

"Yes, you're quiet right, Rhys. If Stratton kept that rendezvous—and I presume you think he did—"

"Well, it would look that way, sir. It's all very well for

him to swear that he backed out of the rendezvous at the last minute, but if she was making trouble for him I think he'd have wanted to see the thing through."

"I'm inclined to agree with you. But what about our recurring red herring? Once again we're presented with the problem of Miss Anne Stratton."

"Well, if we believe Stratton, sir, she wouldn't have had time to meet Miss St. Cellan before bumping into her brother."

"True. So we're back to the original question: how far do we believe Stratton?"

"Not very far, sir, if you ask me. I think he's lying about his sister because he doesn't want her to get cooped for something he did, and I'm sure he's lying when he says he never met the deceased."

"But where's the proof?"

Rhys sighed and folded his hands gently over his stomach. "It'll just be a matter of time, sir. He'll slip up in the end."

"Hmm." Davies rubbed his nose reflectively. "It's a pity about the new Mrs. Stratton, though."

"Yes, sir, she seemed a nice pretty little thing. A shame she ever got mixed up with a smooth customer like Stratton. I wonder how it happened."

"Somebody said they met in America."

"Oh well," said Rhys. "Anything can happen there . . ."

FOUR

After the police left Guy went upstairs to his room where Jenny was waiting for him. She was sitting on the edge of the bed, but as he opened the door she stood up and stubbed out her cigarette.

"Was it all right?" she said at once. Her lips felt oddly stiff so that asking even the simplest question was difficult.

"I don't know." Guy wandered over to the bed, picked up the packet of cigarettes which she had left lying there, and shook one free. All he said when she handed him her lighter was, "The hell with not smoking. This somehow seems the wrong moment to practice self-denial."

"You gave it up for over a year. That's more than most people can do." Even while she spoke half of her mind was amazed that with Guy in such trouble all they could discuss was giving up smoking.

Guy had inhaled from his cigarette and was making a face. "Disgusting!" He stubbed out the cigarette but then changed his mind and relit the tip again. Jenny thought she had never before seen him so restless. "I don't know whether they believed me or not," he said at last. "But I do know they can't prove anything."

"Are you sure?" The uncertainty suddenly seemed unendurable.

"Of course I'm sure!" he exclaimed, glancing at his watch. "I wish Roger would call back about Anne. He was going to phone from the Laurels nursing home as soon as she was settled—ah, there's his car! He must have decided to deliver the news in person." And the cigarette was stubbed out a second time before he hurried downstairs.

The next two hours seemed unending to Jenny. Guy borrowed the Cortina and drove over to the nursing home where Grace had stayed with Anne, and soon after that

Ted went off to work at his father's pub. Aware of her fatigue Jenny tried to sleep, but found it impossible. When Guy returned at last she hoped he would suggest that they take a walk, but Guy wanted only to rest. That night though they both slept badly despite their exhaustion, and the next morning when Jenny stared into the mirror her face looked white and pinched.

After breakfast Guy decided he had to visit Anne again, and although Jenny volunteered to go with him—anything, she thought desperately, would be preferable to Marguerite's curiosity and the four walls of the spare room—he refused to hear of it.

"Grace will be coming with me," he said.

"Can't I come as well?"

"But Jenny, what on earth for? Besides I have business to discuss with Grace and—"

"Forget it," said Jenny, well aware that she wasn't wanted, but Guy did not even hear the bitterness in her voice, and after he left she grabbed her coat and ran outside.

The sun shone fitfully. The landscape was clearly etched in the changing light, and the vast expanse of sands rolled to the distant cliffs. Deliberately avoiding the beach, Jenny began to walk up the cart track which curved around the foot of the Downs, and forty minutes later she was wandering down the high street in search of a shop where she could buy a morning paper.

She was about to enter the news agent's when the door swung open and someone bumped into her.

"Whoa there!" Leonard, looking disreputable in a dirty beige sweater and faded khaki slacks, steadied her apologetically. "Hullo love, come to read all about the tragedy? Tell you what. Save your money and come and have some tea with me. Then you can read my paper while the kettle's coming to the boil."

"That's very kind of you." Jenny found Leonard's practical manner enormously cheering.

"Well, come on, then," said Leonard, "don't let's hang around here, or before you can say another bloody word you'll have all the locals hanging out of their windows to gape at you as if you were a ruddy film star. By the way did you get any visitors from the press yesterday?"

"They rang up but Marguerite left the phone off the hook after the first call, and when they came in person Guy refused to let any of them in."

"I thought they had a frustrated look in the bar last night. Poor devils! What a way to have to earn a living."

Jenny said nervously, "Did you give them an interview?"

Leonard laughed. "What for? I didn't have anything to tell them! All I said was that Emma had been at the pub the night she was killed and they knew that anyway. That fool Charles had been shouting the information from the rooftops."

"You mean Charles told the press—"

"—that Emma had an assignation with Guy."

"But that's not true!" cried Jenny in panic.

"No, I know it's not true, love," said Leonard soothingly. "Emma might have liked the idea but Guy would never have been stupid enough to agree to it. Why Charles had to tell a story like that I can't think—someone ought to knock some sense into his thick head." But as an afterthought he added, "Can't be too harsh on the poor bastard, though, because after all she was his sister. Very close they were too. Poor Emma."

"I suppose you'd known her a long time," said Jenny.

"Yes, I'd known her since I first came to Cellanporth."
They had reached the pub. Whistling jauntily Leonard led
the way to the back door where the aroma of fried bacon
floated from the kitchen to meet them. "Yes," said Leonard, removing a saucepan so that Jenny could sit down at
the kitchen table, "we used to pass the time of day together now and then." He lit the gas and banged the kettle down on the ring. "I rather fancied her, as a matter of
fact. I like that classy, bitchy type—can't think why . . .
still, I had competition with Emma. She was more confused than she realized. I always told her that. 'Oh hell,
Len,' she would say, 'why should I want to be straightened out when I have so much fun?' And I would tell her,
'That's what Christina used to say, and look what happened to her.' "

He was motionless. Jenny could not see his face, but
when he turned a second later she found that he was
smiling.

"The hell with all that," he said cheerfully. "You don't
want to hear about how I played father figure to lost girls.
Or do you? You look a bit of a lost girl yourself. What's
been going on at the Rectory? Ted filled me in with a few
details last night but he didn't seem to know much aside
from the fact that the police had asked the usual routine
questions and got the usual routine nowhere."

"Did the police question you?" said Jenny, wishing he
would talk more about Emma.

"Uh-huh." Leonard yawned. "Same old act. 'Where
were you on the night in question, Mr. Matthews?' 'Visiting a lady friend, Inspector.' 'Could we have her name
and address, Mr. M.?' 'You could, Inspector, but it won't
help you because my car got a puncture on the road to
Porthmawgan and by the time I'd sweated around and

changed the tire I felt too bloody worn out for fun and games.' 'So what did you do then, Mr. M.?' 'I went home to bed and slept all on my ruddy own, Inspector—how's that for a hard luck story?' 'Very sad indeed, Mr. M.,' says he and then damn me if he doesn't start to talk about Christina and asking me questions about the night of the party."

"But you weren't at the party, were you?" Jenny said startled.

"Why not? I suppose you think I'm too old for parties! What a nerve!"

"No, no, I didn't mean that—"

"I know you didn't, love, only teasing. Yes, I went along to the party after the pub closed. That, I might add, was my mistake. I should have stayed at home . . . Still, there's no sense in going into all that now." He began to shovel tea into the pot. "Do you take sugar? I forget."

"No, thanks."

He fidgeted absentmindedly with the milk bottle. "I'll miss Emma . . . Wonder what'll happen to the boutique. That was a white elephant, if you ask me. I told her not to buy it but of course she didn't listen—only turns up on my birthday with a huge box and says sweetly, 'From the boutique, Len dear, to make you look just a tiny bit smarter than you do at present.' And inside the box is this ruddy awful sweater. 'It's absolutely unique,' she says, 'You'll never see another one like it.' 'Thank God for that,' says I, but the next time I see Charles he's wearing one too and it turns out the bloody things were surplus stock that no one wanted. All I can say is that if that was an example of their taste I'm only surprised the shop didn't go bust. Okay, love, tea's coming up—how about a biscuit to fatten you up?"

"No thanks, just tea will be fine."

"You're dying to open up the paper and read all about Emma, aren't you? Go on, don't let me stop you!"

But before Jenny could reply the back door opened and Ted walked into the kitchen to join them.

FIVE

"Hullo," he said surprised to Jenny. "What are you doing here?"

"What are *you* doing here?" said Leonard smartly before Jenny could speak. "Since when have you taken to working on Sundays?"

"I wondered how the village was reacting to the news today."

"How do you think? Gossiping away behind their lace curtains, reassuring themselves that the Wages of Sin is Death. Tea?"

"No thanks." Ted wandered restlessly back to the door. "Have those journalists been back?"

"No, I expect Charles is entertaining them too bloody well at Trecellan Hall."

Ted grimaced and opened the door. "I think I'm going to go for a long walk." He turned as an afterthought to Jenny. "Would you like to come with me? If the tide's right we could go all the way to the end of the Snake's Tail. How about it? Would you like to?"

"Go ahead," said Leonard kindly. "Don't mind me. I'll make some more tea for you later when you get back."

"Well, since you've gone to all the trouble to make tea for me now—"

"I'd have made it for myself anyway. Don't worry,

love, escape if you want to before all those reporters pounce on you for a story."

"I suppose they'll try and get into the house again," Jenny said as they left the pub. "Have you seen a paper yet today?"

"Only the stuffy one Mother had in her room. That had very little about Emma in it—just the fact that she had been found dead on the beach."

They were out on the headland now, past the board with its warning notice, past the last field, and past the highest point of the cliffs. After that the path started to slope downward, and below them in a jagged natural causeway lay the rocks which linked the mainland to the Snake's Tail at low water.

"We'd better check the tides," said Ted, stopping by the coast guard's hut, but luck favored them. The causeway was to be uncovered for the next two hours.

"Getting across is a scramble," warned Ted. "And it takes longer than you'd think. Are your shoes all right for crawling over the rocks?"

"They'll be fine." As they followed the path she watched the sea foaming at the base of the cliffs. "This is much better than sitting at the Rectory and waiting for the police to come back," she remarked presently.

"Yes, isn't it?" Ted seemed to find the idea of waiting at the Rectory as distasteful as she did. "Apparently the police spent yesterday evening interviewing the villagers to find out if anyone saw Emma that night." He kicked a pebble angrily down the path. "I'm just afraid they're going to try to pin the crime on Anne."

"I don't see how they can," said Jenny at once. "She has an alibi."

"But Guy was lying, wasn't he?"

Jenny's heart almost stopped beating. "Why on earth should you think that?"

"Oh . . ." Ted shrugged. "I know Guy would do anything to protect Anne. He wouldn't think twice about lying to the police."

Jenny remembered then that Ted had been with Guy when Christina's body was discovered and had seen Guy remove the threads from her fingernail.

"Guy and I are allies as far as Anne's concerned," Ted said after a moment. Jenny thought he wasn't going to say anything else but he added, "We had so little time together. It was all so bloody unfair."

"But you must have known her at least three years— since your mother married her father."

"Anne was just a kid then. I didn't take much notice of her. It was only after she'd come back from finishing school that I realized . . . well, she was so pretty, so sweet and bright and gay, and . . . I really liked her. Mother wasn't too pleased. She can't help clinging to me because I'm all she's got, but it reached the point where I felt I just had to prove I could stand on my own two feet."

"By taking an interest in Anne?" said Jenny tentatively.

He did not answer immediately. "Anne didn't cling," he said. "She was special. I'd have done anything to keep her safe. Except that I didn't. I let her go to that damn party. I—well, it's no use talking about that now."

They had reached the causeway. It was a jumbled obstacle course of rocks, pools and seaweed, some of the rocks rising to a height of over fifteen feet and some lying prone on the ground like fallen tombstones.

"I'd better lead," said Ted. "I know the easiest route."

Jenny was fascinated by the rock pools. Cool, limpid and serene they reflected the blue of the sky and revealed an intricate word beneath the water's surface, a well-dered world waiting to be transformed by the pulverizing surge of the tide. Several times she stopped, and each time Ted waited patiently until she had caught up with him again.

"Sorry," she apologized at last. "I'm afraid I'm being very slow."

"That's okay. We've got plenty of time."

Jenny glanced around at the sea which was now lapping distantly on both sides of them. "I suppose this could be a dangerous journey if the tide was wrong."

"Yes, you have to be careful. Anne and I were nearly caught once when we came out here for a picnic."

"Ted, about Anne—"

"Yes?"

She still hesitated but curiosity finally won. "Roger Carpenter's in love with her too, isn't he?"

"Roger Carpenter's just an old woman," said Ted with venom. "He'll never get married. Emma used to say to Dad—"

"What?"

"That Roger was undersexed." He tore a strand of seaweed from a nearby rock and shredded it between his fingers. "That's why I get so angry when Roger flutters around Anne—it's all so phony yet no one seems to see that except me."

"But how did Emma get the idea that Roger was undersexed?" said Jenny disbelievingly.

"Because she was so damned vain she thought there was something wrong with any man who didn't make a pass at her. God, how I despised both those St. Cellans! If they hadn't given that party—"

"Were you there?" She did not want to ask questions

which might lead to a discussion of Christina's death, but she found she could not help herself. Part of her shrank from finding out more but part of her remained in the grip of a compulsive desire to know all there was to know.

"Me? At the party?" exclaimed Ted. "I wouldn't have gone to any party given by the St. Cellans. Anne and I quarreled about it—she wanted me to go and I refused, but later that night I missed her so I decided to walk into Cellanporth to see Dad. I wasn't working at the pub then. I was just home for a couple of weeks before the summer term began. Anyway, by the time I got to the pub it was closed. I had a key to the back door so I let myself in and watched television for a bit. A whole crowd from the party came out to dance on the beach and headland, but I just locked the door and turned the television up louder. Later when Dad still wasn't back, I left. The beach party had broken up but I wasn't taking any chances, so I went home through the village and down the cart track. Anne still wasn't back so I sat up and waited. Finally when dawn came I took Mother's car and drove out to Trecellan Hall. You should have seen the place! It was a shambles. There were bodies everywhere—people seemed to have passed out in the most unlikely places. Guy and—" He stopped.

Emma, thought Jenny.

"—and some other people were asleep in the greenhouse. I woke Guy up. I said, 'Where's Anne? Where the *hell* is Anne?' And when he came to he said: 'Isn't she with you?' and that was when I knew something had happened to her. He said, 'We were all at the beach for a while. Maybe she's still there. Or maybe she's somewhere on the headland. Some people said they were going out to the Tail.' And then after a while he said, 'Isn't Christina with you either?' When I said she wasn't he said, 'Oh Lord.' And someone else said, 'Trust Christina,' and he said, 'Shut up.' That was when I had the funny feeling that he still cared—about Christina, I mean—in spite of the fact that . . . well, in spite of the fact that he had obviously got together with Emma at the party.

"We went off to the beach then. Several people had passed out and spent the night there. Christina looked like just another body at first. When we finally realized there was nothing we could do for her, Guy went to fetch Roger and I started looking for Anne again. She was in one of the caves and . . . well, you know the rest."

They had reached dry land once more. Behind them lay the jagged teeth of the causeway, and ahead curled a path which ran along the southern flank of the Snake's Tail.

"I suppose no one could remember what happened to Christina after everyone arrived at the headland," Jenny said slowly.

"Charles said that both Anne and Christina—and some other people—were with him in the Rolls when he left the Hall. He said that when they arrived he lost sight of Anne somehow and went down to the beach to look for her. He doesn't remember seeing either her or Christina again after that."

"Wasn't there some man with Christina? She must have met someone she fancied by that stage of the party."

"As far as I can remember from what was said afterwards, there was someone from London but he'd dropped out before the party moved to the beach." He squashed a nearby cluster of wildflowers with a swipe of his foot. "I don't know how Guy stood the way Christina carried on.

If I'd been him, I wouldn't have cared how much money she had. I'd have left her."

Something in Jenny's expression stopped him. He said awkwardly, "I don't mean that Guy stayed with her just for her money, but after all they both had pretty expensive tastes and Guy always did like the good life."

Jenny heard herself say stiff-lipped, "Architects get good salaries."

"Uh-huh," said Ted. He had turned to look back at the jagged coastline of the bay, and presently Jenny turned too.

"You mustn't listen to me," said Ted after a moment. "I never did like Guy that much, and I suppose it shows sometimes. I'm sorry.'"

All Jenny could bring herself to say was, "But why don't you like him?"

"Well, it's odd," said Ted with a candor which was as unnerving as it was unexpected, "but no matter how sincere and honest he seems to be, I can never believe a single word he says. . . ."

9

ONE

Marguerite looked out of the window and saw them coming across the beach. They were walking close together and for a moment she could picture them hand in hand. It was such an ordinary sight, the young couple strolling across the wide arc of golden sand, both of them attractive to look at, both much the same age, both obviously enjoying themselves . . .

Moving abruptly into the kitchen she glanced out of the window up the track leading to the village. Still no sign of Guy and Grace. That was odd. They could hardly have spent the entire morning visiting Anne.

She began to check on lunch. Despite a succession of interrupting journalists the casserole was almost ready. Better not to do anything about the peas yet. She could start cooking them when Guy and Grace arrived.

The front door opened, Ted called, "Mother? We're back!" and the next moment Jenny was in the kitchen and saying she did hope they weren't late for lunch.

"No, that's quite all right," said Marguerite graciously. "As it happens Guy and Grace aren't back yet. I can't think what they can be doing with themselves in Porth-

mawgan." She glanced into the empty hall. Assorted
noises from upstairs told her that Ted was tidying himself
in his room, and on an impulse she closed the kitchen
door and said to the girl in her pleasantest voice, "I didn't
know you and Ted had planned an outing together this
morning. He didn't mention it at breakfast."

"We met by chance in Cellanporth," said Jenny uneasily, and then wondered amazed if Ted always gave an
advance account of his movements to his mother.

"Oh, I see." Marguerite took another look at the potatoes. "How nice. But I expect Ted seems very young to
you, doesn't he?"

Jenny recognized the drift of the conversation but had
difficulty believing she was not mistaken. She wanted to
say angrily to Marguerite, "What exactly are you suggest-
ing?" But it was so much easier merely to stare at her in
silence, and besides, she had been intimidated by Marguerite from the moment they had met.

"Of course," said Marguerite, suddenly vitriolic, "I
suppose it was too much to hope Guy wouldn't marry a
second Christina. If a man likes a particular type of
woman he tends to choose it over and over again. I knew
he'd have to marry for money since he'd got himself into
such debt though Christina's extravagances and Anne's
medical care—" she did not see Jenny's expression
"—but it's a pity all the same that this time he couldn't at
least find someone with Christina's background."

Jenny was so stunned by this attack that she could not
immediately reply. For a moment all she could think
about was the careless acceptance of the fact that Guy
had married her for her money. Then she cried out, "And
what was *your* background like when you married Leon-

ard? Or are you going to try to make me believe you married far, far beneath you?"

Marguerite turned a most unbecoming shade of red. "I can't see what that has to do with the conversation."

"And *I* can't see why you should accuse me of flirting with Ted and behaving like a second Christina!" flared Jenny, and then as soon as she had spoken she saw it all.

She gasped.

Marguerite regained her pallor with remarkable rapidity and they looked at one another for a long moment. Jenny had just opened her mouth to speak when Marguerite sank down on the nearest chair, leaned her elbows on the kitchen table and covered her eyes with her hands. At last she managed to say, "My dear, I'm so sorry . . . I've no idea what came over me . . . all the strain—the police—and then seeing you and Ted together, walking across the sands . . . It reminded me of how he had once gone for a walk with Christina—"

"But Ted surely didn't find Christina irresistible! He never once hinted that to me!"

"Ted's a very good boy," said Marguerite at once. "He has a lot of common sense and naturally he found Christina's advances absolutely repellent. But I didn't know that at the time. All I knew was that Christina was amusing herself by flirting with him whenever Guy's back was turned. I was worried to death." She stood up again, moved back to the stove and jabbed at a boiling potato with a fork. She was no longer looking at Jenny. When she spoke it was as if she were talking to herself.

"After all," she said, "Ted's my responsibility—I've had to bring him up single-handed—I know some people might say it was wrong for me to have interfered, but . . .

well, I found I simply had to do something. I went to her
and said, 'While you're living under my roof the least you
can do is to keep your hands off my son.' But she just
laughed. She said, 'If you had any real love and respect
for Ted you'd stop treating him as if—' No, I can't bring
myself to repeat what she said. She was sitting in front of
the mirror in the spare room, brushing her hair as she
talked. I was furious but I kept my temper and pleaded,
'You don't love him. Leave him alone. He's only a boy—
you'll hurt him. And suddenly it was *she* who lost
her temper. She flung down her brush and stood up so
violently that she knocked over the dressing table stool.
She screamed that she did love Ted, that he was the only
sweet decent honest person she'd met in years, and she
was crazy about him. And then she said all kinds of
dreadful things, lies, about how I wanted to ruin Ted . . .
I hadn't realized until then what a destructive horrible
creature she was. It was *she* who was determined to ruin
Ted! In the end I managed to say, 'Leave my house tomorrow and never, never come back.' And the ironic part
was that she never did come back to the Rectory again
because that was the night she died . . .

"You know, it's a terrible thing to say, but I was glad
she was dead, glad for Guy, for Ted, for myself. It's a
wicked thing to say, isn't it, but it's the truth." Carefully
laying down the fork Marguerite turned off the gas,
reached for her oven glove and lifted the saucepan from
the stove.

As the steaming water drained into the sink Jenny said,
"You must have been so relieved that Ted didn't go to the
party that night."

"Yes, I was, but when he went out later to see his father I thought he had changed his mind and I stayed up

worrying about him. I wished someone could have been there to talk to me—I was feeling so wretched—but there was no one, all the others were at the party and of course Grace didn't live with us then." She began to pound the potatoes to pulp. "I'm sorry," she said at last. "I really didn't mean to talk so much about Christina to you. It was just that my nerves are all on edge, and . . . oh, I don't know!" She gave Jenny a bright brittle smile. "Do forgive me—Was that a car door slamming? That must be Guy and Grace at last. I was beginning to wonder what had happened to them."

But the door belonged not to the car but to Ted's room upstairs. Presently Ted himself appeared in the kitchen in search of lunch, and although Jenny moved to the back door in the vain hope that Marguerite had not been mistaken, the courtyard was still empty.

TWO

"Guy," said Grace as they left the Laurels Nursing Home at Porthmawgan soon after noon, "may I have a word in private with you before we get back to the Rectory?"

Guy's heart sank. "Of course." They were sitting in Marguerite's car and he had been about to switch on the engine before Grace had forestalled him. The trees in the nursing home grounds drooped moistly beneath gray skies and the Queen Anne mansion which housed the patients looked heavy and somber in the dull light.

"Guy, I know you have a lot on your mind, but I've been thinking of the future and I really believe—"

"You can't possibly give in your notice now," said Guy

roughly. "Especially after Roger's just told us that Anne should be better in a couple of weeks and ready to come home again."

"Roger takes a very optimistic view of the case, if you want my opinion on the subject. He believes only what he wants to believe. He shouldn't really be consulted in Anne's case at all, you know—he's much too emotionally involved."

Guy said nothing but leaned forward again to switch on the ignition.

"I would still prefer to give notice, Guy," Grace persisted. "I've wanted to for a long time but I didn't like to leave you in the lurch."

"I'll give you more money."

"It's not the money, Guy. It's just that I feel I'm not getting anywhere by staying here. I must move on."

The engine sprang to life but Guy made no move to set the car in motion.

"Getting anywhere?" he repeated. "You mean in your career?"

"In my personal life."

Guy was startled. He had never imagined Grace having any secrets. "Well, I have no right to ask about that, of course," he said after a pause, "but—"

"Why not? You confided in me once about your personal life—remember? On the afternoon of the day Christina died we went for that walk together and you poured out all your troubles to me."

Guy looked embarrassed. "I always regretted that afterwards. God knows what possessed me to moan like that about my job and my wife and my debts!"

"I was glad you felt able to confide in me, and besides I

was pleased to listen to someone complain about Christina."

Guy was more startled than ever. "What did you have against Christina?"

"She was playing around with someone I liked. Guy, do we have to sit here with the engine running?"

Guy automatically began to drive away from the nursing home. "You mean there was someone who——"

"Well, why else do you suppose I've chosen to bury myself in Cellanporth all this time? However, I might just as well not have bothered. He'll never look at me twice, that's plain. I'm not his type. Christina, Emma—yes. But not me."

"You're not by any chance talking about——"

"Never mind who I'm talking about," said Grace fiercely. "It doesn't matter any more anyway because I'm determined to go away and start afresh somewhere else."

They were in Porthmawgan by this time and Guy, ignoring the signpost to Cellanporth, swung off the road onto a track which led to the dunes.

"Where are you going?" Grace said sharply.

"Nowhere. I just want to park the car. I can't talk about something like this and drive at the same time." As he spoke the track dissolved into a valley between two enormous grassy banks, and he braked to a halt. The fronds of grass on the dunes swayed delicately in the sea breeze, and the gulls soared dreamily above the skyline.

Presently Guy said, "Will you wait two weeks? Then if Anne's still in the nursing home you can leave as soon as you want to."

"Well . . ."

"Good God, Grace, if you've waited all this time you

might just as well wait two weeks longer! It would mean a great deal to me—and to Anne too. Say you'll stay. Please."

"Oh, all right!" She sounded furious with herself for giving in. "You win!" And when she refused to look at him he realized she was angry with him too for persuading her to stay.

There was an awkward silence. Then, "Well, what on earth are we doing still sitting here?" said Grace annoyed. "For God's sake let's go back to Cellanporth and have some lunch."

Guy made no attempt to argue but merely turned the car and headed back to the road. He was feeling exhausted. His sole ambition at that moment was to fall into bed and sleep all afternoon.

At the Rectory they found that Marguerite and Ted were already clearing the dirty dishes from the dining room. The remains of the casserole sat on top of the stove.

"I'm so sorry, Guy," said Marguerite, "but rather than ruin the meal we decided to go ahead and eat. I hope you don't mind."

"Of course not. Where's Jenny?"

"She went off somewhere. She didn't say where. Shall I dish up lunch for you now?"

But all Guy said was, "I'm sorry, but I'm not hungry. Could you tell Jenny when she comes in that I'm upstairs resting? I feel very tired."

But he was unable to sleep. At three o'clock he left the house and walked toward Cellanporth in search of his wife.

THREE

Roger Carpenter too had had a difficult morning. He had made his regular visit to Porthmawgan cottage hospital, and from there he had gone to the Laurels to see Anne and confer with Guy and Grace. Anne worried him; she had been totally withdrawn, refusing to speak. But despite Grace's obvious pessimism, he felt there was no reason why Anne should not recover sufficiently within a week or two to be able to leave the nursing home—and no reason why she should not ultimately make a total recovery.

Nonetheless Roger felt tired after his morning's work, and when he arrived home he was relieved to find few patients had phoned in his absence. He was still examining the list of calls when his housekeeper knocked on the door of his consulting room and informed him gloomily that the "new Mrs. Guy Stratton" was waiting to see him in the living room.

"Jenny!" said Roger startled.

"And your lunch is ready, doctor." The housekeeper sounded as if she fully expected him not to eat it.

"Good," said Roger vaguely. "I won't be long." And leaving the list of calls on his desk he hurried at once to the living room.

Jenny was sitting on the edge of the sofa. Her face was so pale that her freckles stood out sharply, and her hands twisted at the rings on her wedding finger.

"Hullo!" he said guardedly, sensing her distress. "What a nice surprise! Can I get you a drink?"

"No, thanks. Roger, I just felt I had to talk to someone and you were the only person I could think of. Can I talk to you as if you were a doctor? I mean——" She was having trouble explaining. "——I mean, can I talk to you in confidence?"

"Of course," he said soothingly, and sat down beside her on the sofa.

But she did not know how to begin. She went on fidgeting with her rings and staring unhappily at the carpet until he said, "You're probably still recovering from the shock of finding Emma's body. Did you manage to sleep much last night?"

"Not much, no."

"I'll prescribe a sedative for you, if you like."

"No, I . . . Roger, I didn't come here to talk about that. I wanted to talk to you about Guy."

He suppressed his immediate twinge of anxiety. "Yes?"

"What I wanted to know was . . . is Anne's medical care very expensive?"

"Yes, in some respects," he said startled. "The Laurels is a private nursing home, and Grace has a right to a first class salary. I myself make no charges although I must confess I treat Anne as I would a private patient. But she's registered with me under the National Health scheme, just as most of my other patients are."

"But how can Guy afford Grace and the Laurels? I know he has a good salary but Marguerite says Christina got him into debt——"

"Oh, I wouldn't take anything Marguerite says about Christina too seriously, if I were you. There was no love lost between them."

"Yes, Marguerite told me just now that Christina was infatuated with Ted——" She stopped when she saw Roger's expression. "Well, wasn't she?"

"It was Ted who was infatuated with Christina!"

Against his better judgment Roger felt his air of professional detachment evaporating. He realized dimly that he had wanted to talk to someone since Anne had returned to the nursing home. "That boy's got a lot to answer for," he heard himself say sharply. "If you want my opinion on the subject, he's more than a little to blame for Anne's illness. She had a schoolgirl crush on him when she came home from Switzerland, but when Guy came to visit the Rectory it became obvious that Ted was infatuated with Christina and that Christina was doing everything possible to egg him on. Anne must have been dreadfully hurt. I think she decided that if she wanted Ted to take more notice of her she would have to be more like Christina and that was why, when she got to that damn party, she tried to act the part of city sophisticate. There's no other reason why she would have tried LSD." He managed to stop himself. He was about to apologize for taking control of the conversation in such an emotional fashion when Jenny said slowly, "I thought she took LSD by accident."

He realized then that she was anxious to prolong the diversion and he wondered if she were already regretting confiding in him. "Frankly, no one knows how she came to take the drug," he answered after a moment. "I know Guy's theory is that Charles slipped it into her drink for a joke, but I don't believe even Charles St. Cellan would have played such a filthy trick. It doesn't fit in with my knowledge of his character. He would have offered Anne the drug quite openly and if she'd refused it he would have moved on to someone else."

Jenny still made no effort to change the subject. "How much does Anne remember?"

"It's hard to know." He sighed. "She gets upset if she's questioned about the party, and her memory of the entire evening is obviously very confused. Sometimes I wish I shared some of her amnesia, but I remember the evening all too clearly." He stood up and moved restlessly to the window. "I was called out that night," he said. "An old woman who lives three doors from the pub was ill and I walked over from my house to see her. On my way home I saw several cars tear through the village toward the headland. I remember thinking as I watched everyone reeling out of them that I'd probably get a call later, but I never dreamed that the victims would be Anne and Christina." He clasped his hands tightly together and watched the skin whiten over his knuckles. Then in an effort to regain his professional composure he turned abruptly from the window and said with regret, "I'm sorry, I'm not being much help. You wanted to discuss Guy, not Anne."

"It's two sides of the same story," she said unexpectedly. "I see that now." She too stood up. "I'd better get back to the Rectory."

He felt that he had failed her in some way. "Has Guy given you some reason to believe he's in financial trouble?" he asked quickly.

"No," she said. "But there's so much Guy never tells me . . . Roger, did he pay back that loan you made him?"

He jumped. "Yes, he did. God, how did you know about the loan?" And then he saw, too late, that she had been guessing.

"When did he pay it back?"

"Look, Jenny—"

"When?"

"Oh . . . about three weeks ago. He sent me a check."

"Was it drawn on our joint account?"

"I don't remember," he lied, but she recognized the lie at once and became paler than ever. He felt angry then, angry with himself for lying, angry with Guy for using his wife's money in such a secretive fashion, angry with Jenny for underlining his friend's less attractive qualities. "Guy's had a lot of worries during the past year or two," he said, trying to sound calm. "I'm sure everything will straighten out in time."

"Oh yes," she said. "I expect so." She turned to the door again and this time he made no effort to detain her. Instead he escorted her outside to the garden gate and watched her start walking back to the Rectory.

FOUR

Halfway home Jenny climbed on top of one of the rocks at the side of the lane and sat for a while facing the sea. It was no longer cloudy. At the foot of the cliffs below Cellanporth morbid sightseers were still wandering around the sand where Emma's body had been found, and Jenny turned her head away sharply from the sight of them. She did not want to think of Emma. She did not even want to think of Guy, for that allowed her no chance to escape from her worst fears.

He would have an explanation, of course. "Darling, I didn't want to bother you with money matters . . . I wanted to repay Roger—such an old friend . . . our best man . . . after all, you did say you wished your money was a dowry and that you felt guilty about inheriting it from Harlan . . . I didn't think you'd mind. . . ."

No, thought Jenny, I wouldn't have minded. I still

don't mind except that I wish you could have told me
about it instead of acting behind my back.

She felt it implied a lack of trust on Guy's part, and
somewhere, far away at the back of her mind, lurked the
tight dark thought: supposing he really did only marry me
for the money.

She was still staring blindly down at the sightseers on
the beach when she heard Guy call her name. Twisting
around she saw him hurrying up the cart track toward
her.

"Jenny, are you all right?" He sounded anxious. "Is
anything the matter?"

Not long ago she would have told him frankly enough
what the matter was, but now she found she could no
longer be honest.

"Nothing's the matter," she said flatly. "I just went for
a walk."

"You look as if you'd been worrying yourself silly," he
said concerned. "I wish to God I could think of something to do which would take our minds off this whole
damn business! I hate the idea of sitting around waiting
for the police to return—and I'm sure they *will* return
sooner or later. If I spend the next few hours wondering
what questions they'll ask me, I'll go out of my mind.
Look—I've got an idea. Perhaps if Marguerite has no ob-
jection we could have a small dinner party. Why don't I
call Roger and ask him to come over?"

Jenny opened her mouth to say that attending a dinner
party was the last way she wanted to spend the evening,
but she changed her mind. Perhaps Guy was right and the
presence of other people would help to ease the tension.

"That sounds like a good idea," she said slowly. "Yes, ask Roger."

"Maybe Leonard could come over too. He's always good company and since it's Sunday the pub will be closed."

"Marguerite won't want to invite him, will she?" said Jenny, but when they reached the Rectory they found that Marguerite was as eager as Guy to be diverted from all thought of the police; she even offered to telephone her ex-husband herself. The only problem lay in finding enough food at such short notice to make a presentable dinner for seven. Fortunately Marguerite prided herself on the excellence of her housekeeping and was able to produce several large tins of pheasant in a wine sauce before she retired to the kitchen to prepare an enormous bowl of apple charlotte for pudding.

"Leonard said he would bring some wine," she said. "I hope he doesn't forget. He always becomes very absent-minded if he has to contribute something to a party."

But Leonard remembered and arrived promptly at seven o'clock with two bottles of gloomy-looking Beaujolais from some forgotten corner of his cellar, and a cunning array of stories calculated to shock Marguerite and amuse the others. Roger, the only other guest from the village, found he could hardly get a word in edgeways, but he seemed content to remain a listener as he sipped his whiskey at one end of the sofa.

They were just finishing the main course when the front door bell rang.

Guy said much too quickly, "I suppose that's the police."

"Oh my Gawd," said Leonard and poured himself some more wine.

"At eight o'clock on a Sunday night?" Marguerite protested. "Surely not!"

"It's probably the press," Ted said. "I thought they'd got bored with trying to blitz their way in here but maybe they decided to have one more try."

"Well, don't let's all just sit here!" said Grace. "Let's see who it is and what they want." And she stood up, marched out into the hall and flung open the door.

There was a silence. In the dining room everyone was very still.

"My dear Grace!" the visitor drawled at last. "How are you? I say, may I come in? I have a little message to deliver to your charming employer." And before Grace had even had time to reply Charles St. Cellan had stepped neatly past her and was strolling nonchalantly into the dining room.

FIVE

Guy stood up. "What the hell do you want?"

"My dear chap, what a reception!"

"What kind of reception do you expect to get after all those lies you told the press?"

"If you mean my comments on your rendezvous with Emma—"

"You know damned well that's what I mean!"

"Well, I only said that she'd arranged to meet you! My God, anyone would think I said you killed her." Charles glanced casually around the guests at the table and Jenny realized that he was enjoying himself. It was the enjoyment of a man who thrived on danger. Charles' long love affair with death was aflame once more after a prolonged period of apathy.

"I never met Emma that night," said Guy, "and you were a bloody fool to hold an open house for the press like that. Make one more insinuation and I'm seeing my solicitors."

"But my dear fellow, I didn't come here tonight to argue. I hoped we could have a friendly private chat. No, don't tell me to go to hell! I think it would be in your best interests to listen."

"Drop it, Charlie," said Leonard. "It's the wrong time and the wrong place. Try Hollywood twenty years ago."

"It's all right, Leonard," said Guy wearily. "I know he's ridiculous but it would be selfish of me to let him ruin the entire dinner party." He stood up and added to Charles without looking at him, "You'd better come into the living room."

"No thanks," said Charles. "There's too much risk of being overheard. How about the kitchen?"

Guy evidently thought the suggestion was too melodramatic to merit a comment. As Jenny watched nervously he led the way out into the hall, but it was not until he had gone that she realized how close she was to panic.

"Well, really!" Marguerite was saying scandalized. "What an extraordinary exhibition of bad taste!"

Ted said succinctly, "He's crazy," and helped himself to more vegetables.

"I expect he's still suffering from the shock of his sister's death," murmured Roger, offering the conventional charitable explanation.

"Grief," said Grace severely, "is no excuse for bad manners."

"Charlie hardly struck me as being in a state of shock," said Leonard. "He was having a bloody good time and didn't mind who knew it . . . Is there any more wine?"

"You've just drunk the last drop," said Marguerite coldly. "Have some more vegetables, Roger. I can't fetch the pudding until Guy and Charles are finished in the kitchen."

The confrontation must have been brief. After five minutes Guy returned alone and to Jenny's confusion she saw that his anger was now mixed with bewilderment.

"Well, do tell us," said Marguerite. "What was it all about? Or shouldn't I ask?"

"By all means ask." Guy sat down at the table again and glancing at Jenny gave her a brief nod of reassurance. "If he thought I would be too gripped with guilt to repeat his preposterous theories, he's miscalculated. I'm not guilty and I don't give a damn if you all know. He's quite mad, of course."

"Yes, but Guy dear, what did he *say?*"

"In a nutshell he thinks I killed Christina. He's already convinced that I killed Emma, but as far as Christina's concerned he says that Anne's convinced him that Christina's death was no accident and that I was responsible. I suppose everyone here knows by now how Anne identified Charles as a murderer; it's Charles' theory that Anne mistook him for me—Charles and I are physically not unalike and Anne wasn't wearing her glasses. I must say, it's a plausible theory but it does have one major flaw. It's absolutely wrong."

"My dear Guy, you don't have to tell us that!" exclaimed Roger. "Besides, I feel very strongly that Anne was hallucinating at the time and no importance should be attached to what she said."

"Exactly what I told Charles, but of course he wasn't going to accept anything which would undermine his precious theory."

Leonard puffed a smoke ring at the ceiling. "Did Emma know about it?"

"Apparently it was her idea—and the reason why she wanted to meet me on the cliff that night. She was going to sound me out. Of course as soon as Charles heard Emma was dead he immediately thought she'd tricked me into betraying myself and that I'd killed her to keep her quiet."

"Monstrous!" cried Marguerite fascinated.

"But surely Charles himself must have realized that Anne's statement proved nothing!" exclaimed Roger.

"He was certainly anxious to get more concrete proof. That was why, when he met Anne wandering outside the pub, he took her back to Trecellan Hall. He wanted time to question her. He only succeeded in upsetting her, of course, but—"

"My God," muttered Roger, "I could—" He bit the words off before they could be spoken.

"Shall I help you bring in the pudding, Mrs. Stratton?" offered Grace, trying to ease the situation.

"Thank you, dear," said Marguerite and they left the room.

Jenny suddenly found she could speak again. "But Guy," she said in a rush, "what was the point of Charles' visit just now? Why did he make such an elaborate production of telling you his suspicions in private?"

"I think he was trying to give me enough rope to hang myself," Guy said dryly. "According to the book of rules

I should now try to kill him before he goes to the police. However, much as I should like to oblige him I'm afraid he's going to be disappointed."

SIX

After dinner everyone began to drink again. Guy was mixing strong scotch and sodas for the men and equally strong gin and tonics for the women, but at ten Marguerite and Grace withdrew to the kitchen to clear up. Jenny offered to help, but Marguerite, perhaps in an attempt to make amends for her previous outburst of temper, insisted that Jenny was on holiday and should not be burdened with chores.

Jenny drifted back to the living room. By this time she was relaxed, even indifferent to Guy's danger. She had not drunk so much for a long while.

Later Marguerite and Grace returned to the living room, but after another round of drinks they excused themselves and went upstairs to bed. Thinking that the men would prefer to be on their own, Jenny tried to follow, but Leonard and Guy refused to let her leave and she rashly consented to another gin. After that the room became dreamily rosy and the conversation was a river surging over the top of her head. At first she lay curled up on the sofa with her head on Guy's shoulder, but later she realized she had dozed, because when she opened her eyes her head was on Leonard's shoulder and Guy was standing by the fireplace as he gave an imitation of a New York cab driver. Roger was talking at the same time; he seemed to be lecturing Ted on the history of psychoanalysis. At regular intervals he would pause to say, "Of course it's not really my subject. I always specialized in anatomy," and Ted would nod and look solemn.

When she opened her eyes again Guy was depositing her clumsily on their double bed.

"What's happening?" she murmured sleepily.

"I think I'm going to make love to you," said Guy.

But he didn't.

"Goddamned alcohol," growled Guy, and fell asleep with her hand clasped firmly in his and his cheek pressed apologetically against her shoulder.

Jenny slept.

When she awoke the daylight hurt her eyes and her mouth felt as if it were lined with rough towels. It was several minutes before she summoned the courage to open one eyelid a fraction and saw that Guy was still sprawled beside her. He was lying on top of the eiderdown, but at some point during the night he must have roused himself sufficiently to drag the discarded counterpane on top of him to ward off the cold. She was just envying him his deep sleep when there was a knock at the door.

"Come in," she called with an effort.

The door opened. Marguerite, faultlessly groomed as usual, peeped in. "My dear, I do apologize for disturbing you, but I'm afraid you'll both have to wake up."

"Oh?" Jenny tried not to sound as weak as she felt. "Why? What's happened?"

"It's the police," said Marguerite. "They've come back. I've no idea what they want, but they're asking to speak to Guy."

10

"Good morning, Mr. Stratton," said Detective-Inspector Davies with the equanimity which Guy was beginning to know and dread. "Sorry to drag you out of bed, but we're investigating a case of arson and I did just want to have a brief word with you about it."

Guy had until that moment been conscious only of the immense effort needed to keep on his feet, but the word "arson" wiped all thought of physical discomfort from his mind.

He stared at Davies. "Did you say arson?"

"Yes, Mr. Stratton." Davies looked at him with gentle interest. Sergeant Rhys, who had parked his bulk unobtrusively on a chair by the door, gave a small sigh and turned over a page of his notebook.

At last Guy said, "I'm sorry but I'm not feeling very intelligent this morning. Am I supposed to know something about this?"

"Well, you tell us, Mr. Stratton. Do you?"

"I don't know anything about it at all! Where—"

"Trecellan Hall, Mr. Stratton. Someone set fire to the house last night. The place is a total wreck, I'm sorry to

176

say, though Mr. St. Cellan was able to summon the fire
engine very quickly."

"Was St. Cellan all right?"

"He had a mild case of smoke inhalation, but otherwise
he seems fine. The hospital is supposed to discharge him
this morning to stay with friends in Castlesea. Fortunately
the housekeeper was away."

"But why are you certain it was arson? Where was St.
Cellan when the fire started? I don't see how—why—"

"Mr. St. Cellan," said Davies, "was anticipating an attack on his person but not on his property. He had taken
cover in the hall cloakroom which happens to have a fine
view down the drive to the road. He was also armed with
a gun for which, I'm sorry to say, he did not have a li-
cense."

There was a pause. Guy thought of several things to
say, but since none of them would have provided a positive contribution to the conversation he said nothing.

"Apparently he thought you might visit him, Mr. Stratton," said Davies mildly.

"Well, I'm glad someone came even if I didn't," said
Guy, wishing his head would stop aching. "I'd hate to
think of him waiting all night long in a lavatory for nothing. I suppose whoever it was entered the house from the
back."

"Why should you think that?"

"Because," said Guy, wondering in despair which of
them was being stupid and hoping that it was Davies, "if
St. Cellan was watching the front, then his visitor must
have entered the house from some other direction."

"Mr. St. Cellan had the burglar alarms switched on for
every door but the front, and all the downstairs windows
were bolted."

Guy tried to concentrate on the problem but gave up. "So?"

"So?" said Davies.

Sergeant Rhys sighed and turned over another page of his notebook.

"All right," said Guy. "You tell me. I give up. How did the intruder get in? Did he climb up a drainpipe and force one of the upstairs windows?"

"What makes you think he got in at all?"

"But you said—" Guy stopped. He was aware of a small knot of tension forming in his stomach.

"I said Trecellan Hall had been burned down by persons unknown. That's all."

"Yes, but—"

"Ever heard of a Molotov cocktail, Mr. Stratton?"

"Lord, yes. Why, do you mean—"

"Someone tossed a Molotov cocktail through the window of Mr. St. Cellan's bedroom. The noise of the breaking glass and explosion made Mr. St. Cellan dash upstairs —only to find the room on fire. Realizing the danger he telephoned the fire department before he went outside and by that time the culprit had vanished."

"Good God," said Guy, unable to think of anything else to say.

"The arsonist must have approached the house from the Downs. Probably he escaped by the same route." He glanced out of the window. "Trecellan Hall's not far from here as the crow flies, is it?" He slipped his hands casually into his pockets. "A Molotov cocktail is nice and easy to make too. I understand it's very popular with student rioters, especially those that aren't mechanically minded. I've even heard of young girls making them . . . It's a great pity about Trecellan Hall, I must say—and I feel very sorry for Mr. St. Cellan. All his possessions were destroyed and he doesn't even have any clothes except the ones he was wearing at the time of the explosion."

"He was lucky to get out alive," said Guy.

"Possibly," said Davies. "But it seems a haphazard sort of way to try to kill someone, don't you think?"

"You don't believe someone was trying to kill him?"

"I don't know. Mr. St. Cellan believes it all right, but I'm not so sure."

"What other reason would anyone have for chucking a bomb into his bedroom in the middle of the night?"

"Put it this way," said Davies. "Why should anyone have wanted to kill him?"

"To frame me of course." Guy sat down suddenly on the sofa and took a cigarette from the box on the coffee table. "He came here last night, as I'm sure he's told you, to set me up for the role of murderer, and now, I've no doubt he thinks he's succeeded in proving his point. In fact if you want my opinion, I don't believe that story about waiting in the hall cloakroom with a gun. I think he made the bomb himself and tossed it through his own bedroom window."

"You mean he sacrificed his home to frame you?"

"He probably didn't think the fire would spread quickly, but I'm certain he did it to frame me. He thinks I killed his sister but since he couldn't prove it he decided to manufacture the proof itself. It's as plain as a pikestaff."

"Well, it's possible. We'll have to think about that, won't we, Rhys?"

"Yes, sir," said Rhys seriously. "We will."

Damn them, thought Guy, they're worse than a bad vaudeville team. He said abruptly, "If I'd planned any harm to St. Cellan why did I tell everyone at the dinner party last night about his ridiculous theories? Why did I reveal I had a motive for keeping him quiet?"

"Good thinking, Mr. Stratton," said Davies. "But you could have drawn those conclusions while you were showing Mr. St. Cellan out and decided to tell the truth so that everyone would be too impressed by your honesty to suspect you later. That would be quite a neat piece of bluff, wouldn't it? Well now, let's move away from speculation and concentrate on the facts. At about what time did your guests leave last night?"

"I've no idea," said Guy, unnerved by Davies' swift counterattack. "We all drank too much. At least to be accurate some of us drank too much. My stepmother and Miss Reid went up to bed at about eleven, I seem to remember, but Roger Carpenter, Leonard, Ted, and my wife and I sat around down here for a good deal longer. At a guess I'd say it was at least two hours. But it could have been four. Maybe one of the others would remember better than I can."

"And then? Did Mr. Leonard Matthews and Dr. Carpenter leave together?"

"I think so. Yes, they did because Roger offered Leonard a lift. Leonard had walked here across the sands earlier that evening and didn't have his car."

"And after they'd both gone I assume that you and your wife and Mr. Ted Matthews went up to your respective rooms."

"Yes."

"And then?"

"The next thing I knew was your arrival being announced before I had had a chance to breakfast on Alkaseltzer."

"I see. Well, Mr. Stratton, we won't keep you any longer, but I wonder if we could now have a word with your wife?"

TWO

"I've no idea what time Leonard and Roger went," said Jenny, trying to concentrate so minutely on Davies' questions that there was no room left in her mind for fear. "I'm afraid I was asleep by then. I wouldn't even like to guess what time it was."

"You were asleep downstairs?"

"Yes, I dozed off on the sofa. But I woke up when Guy carried me to our room."

"And then what happened?"

"We went to bed." Jenny felt embarrassed. "I suppose we both sort of passed out."

"Who passed out first?" said Davies, as if it were the most natural thing in the world to pass out after a Sunday night dinner party.

"Guy," said Jenny at once.

"Are you sure?"

"Yes. Positive."

"You can remember that?"

"Yes."

"But you can't remember what time it was."

"I didn't look at the clock. But I'm sure about Guy because—" She stopped and to her horror felt herself blush. There was a long awkward pause before Davies prompted, "Yes, Mrs. Stratton?"

"Nothing. Just something personal."

"I'm afraid I'm going to have to ask you to tell us."

Jenny swallowed. "It was just . . . well . . ." She was painfully aware of the sergeant's pencil whispering across the pages of his notebook. "We were going to make love," she heard herself say in a rush. "But Guy . . . we . . . didn't. And then Guy fell asleep. But I remember, you see, because I was all ready to—to . . . and then we didn't."

"Yes, I see," said Davies. "Yes, of course, now I can understand your certainty. Thank you, Mrs. Stratton. Well, I don't think we need trouble you further at present. I wonder if you would be good enough to ask young Mr. Matthews to come in and see us for a moment . . ."

THREE

Later Davies said to his sergeant, "Well, what do you make of it, Rhys? Mrs. Marguerite Stratton says the party broke up at quarter past two when she was awakened by her ex-husband Leonard Matthews singing 'D'ye Ken John Peel?' in the backyard. Miss Reid confirms this, so it looks as if we can take two-fifteen to be correct. Trecellan Hall was burned less than two hours later at four o'clock, and—let's see, how long do you think it would take to walk to the Hall from the Rectory? Twenty minutes? Half an hour? Anyway, if it was someone from the house there was plenty of time. Unless you believe the bomb was thrown by a stray vandal."

"I wouldn't think that was really too likely, sir," said Rhys. "Not considering Mr. St. Cellan's performance at the Rectory when he all but asked to be murdered."

"Yes, but he wasn't murdered, was he?"

"Sheer bad luck, if you ask me, sir. From the murderer's point of view, I mean."

"Rhys, if you'd killed two people and were seriously threatened by a third, would you really employ such a hit-and-miss method?"

"Well, it's all rather curious, sir, I must say. But if the motive for bombing the Hall wasn't to kill Mr. St. Cellan, then just what was the motive?"

"That's exactly it, Rhys. We keep coming back to the original suspects. What are the odds on Stratton now, do you suppose?"

"Lengthening, I'd say, sir. One can disbelieve every word he says, but one can't disbelieve little Mrs. Stratton. She was telling the truth all right, but he could have been faking his stupor."

"True. He was making the drinks. He could have made his own very weak if he was planning a visit to the Hall."

"And not everyone drank till two in the morning. The two who went to bed early were sober enough to have gone out."

"Can you honestly visualize Mrs. Stratton senior mixing a Molotov cocktail, Rhys?"

"Well, I don't know, sir," said Rhys vaguely. "I don't suppose it would be half as complicated as mixing the dye she uses on her hair. And the most surprising people do know about bombs these days. Think of the dowager duchess at the antidisarmament demonstration last month."

"All right, Rhys, you suspect Mrs. Stratton, and the best of luck to you, but personally I believe that whoever blew up Trecellan Hall would have pretended to be as drunk as a lord so that he could escape suspicion later—"

"And that brings us back to Stratton again, doesn't it, sir?"

"Damn Stratton," said Davies. "The more I think about it the more certain I am that he's not being honest with us. For instance, I'm sure—quite sure—he met Emma St. Cellan on the headland and I'm equally sure he didn't speak to his sister when he says he did."

"I thought we'd abandoned Anne Stratton as a suspect, sir?"

"We have. Anne could have killed Christina Stratton and she could, I suspect, have killed Emma St. Cellan, but she didn't set Trecellan Hall on fire last night. The staff at the Laurels can vouch that she never left her bed. Similarly, I can see Stratton killing his wife and his ex-mistress but I can't see him bungling the job of killing Charles St. Cellan. It doesn't add up."

"It must have been Stratton, sir. If we could prove he was lying about meeting Miss St. Cellan that night—"

"It would be a beginning, I agree." Davies sighed. "Well, I hate to do it, but it looks as if we'll have to snap the weak link in the chain, Rhys. You know who I mean, of course."

"Yes, sir," said Rhys. "If Stratton really did meet Miss St. Cellan that night, he's not the only one who's been lying to us."

FOUR

All Jenny could think was, Guy must have woken up in the night because this morning he was sleeping with the counterpane wrapped around him.

She had taken the counterpane from the bed before dinner and left it on the window seat.

Then she thought: Supposing . . .

But Guy would only have wanted to kill Charles if Charles' accusations had been true. And of course she knew he hadn't killed Emma or Christina. So in that case he would hardly have tried to kill Charles.

She almost said to Guy: "It wasn't you, was it?" but she did not want him to know she could have doubted his innocence.

She was still battling with her thoughts when the police returned to the Rectory and, for the second time that morning, asked if they could speak to her alone.

FIVE

"Sorry to trouble you again, Mrs. Stratton," said Davies kindly, "but there are just one or two points that I'd like to go over with you. Won't you sit down?"

Jenny was too tense to reply. She sat down at the dining room table and waited mutely for the interrogation to begin.

"I'd like to go back to the night Emma St. Cellan was killed. What time did you say you and your husband went to bed?"

"Eight o'clock. We decided to have an early night."

"And about what time did you go to sleep?"

"I—I'm not sure. About ten perhaps."

"Did you fall asleep before your husband?"

"Perhaps. Yes, I think I did."

"And you woke up at—"

"Just before Ted came back from the pub. I think it

was getting on for half-past twelve. I woke up, felt thirsty
—I told you this, didn't I?—and decided to go downstairs
to get a drink of water. I met Ted in the hall."

"You were, naturally, astonished to see him."

"Yes, I—" She stopped. He noticed how she twisted
her hands. "Yes, in a way," she said unevenly. "It was
late for him."

"You weren't afraid that someone was breaking in?"

"No, I thought it must be Ted."

"I see. But Ted claims you said in a surprised voice:
'Oh, it's *you!*'—as if you expected it to be someone else."

There was a longer pause. She was twisting her wedding ring now, working it round and round her finger.

"You're sure you didn't think that it was someone else
who had just entered the house?"

"No, because there was no one else it could have been.
I was just surprised because he was later than usual."

"All right, go on. Did you get your drink of water from
the kitchen?"

"No, Grace Reid interrupted us to say Anne was missing."

"Now this is the part that puzzles me, Mrs. Stratton.
Why did no one rush to your room and wake your husband with this rather horrifying piece of news?"

"I went to tell him myself."

"But you didn't, did you, Mrs. Stratton?"

"I—"

"According to the others you were downstairs until
both Ted Matthews and Miss Reid left the house. Mrs.
Marguerite Stratton said she heard you go to your room
while she was dressing, but there was no sound indicating
you had woken your husband."

"Yes, but—"

"Why did you delay so long, Mrs. Stratton? What were you waiting for?"

"I don't know!" cried Jenny. "I—I was frightened—Anne scared me—I couldn't think properly—I just didn't want Guy to go rushing out with the others—I wanted to make sure he stayed with me—I thought the longer I delayed telling him—"

To conceal his annoyance at her plausibility Davies swung around on Rhys. "Ask Mr. Stratton to come in, would you please?"

They waited. Rhys' voice boomed in the hall. A moment later Guy, looking very white around the lips, entered the room.

"Sit down, Mr. Stratton." Davies kept his manner curt. "I've just been asking your wife some further questions about the night of Emma St. Cellan's death, and I regret to say that I find her answers far from satisfactory."

Jenny was trying not to cry. As Davies paused he saw her fumble for a handkerchief, saw Guy sense the depth of her distress, saw his quarry at last with his back to the wall.

"I'm sorry, Mrs. Stratton," he said gently.

Guy turned on him with blazing eyes. "For Christ's sake, can't you leave her alone?"

"I'm only trying to do my job, Mr. Stratton. And my job now obliges me to stress that when even the nicest witnesses begin to lie to the police they don't do themselves one bit of good. I don't think your wife quite realizes the penalties to which she could be liable if—"

"She's not liable for anything!" Guy stood up. "Leave her alone!"

"I'm sorry, sir, but if she persists in lying to the police—"

"I'm the one who lied! It's got nothing to do with her, do you hear? Nothing! She only acted to protect me, and I only lied because—"

"Because you did meet Emma St. Cellan after all," said Davies, "and you didn't think I would ever believe you if you swore on the Bible that in spite of that you didn't kill her."

There was a silence. Jenny had hidden her face in her hands and was crying soundlessly.

My God, thought Davies, I'd like to give him the fright of his life for having put her through this.

"I'm not saying another word unless my solicitor is present," said Guy unevenly.

"You can phone him from the police station in Castlesea."

"You mean—"

"No," said Davies, "I'm not arresting you. If you come with us you come voluntarily, but if you'll take my advice you'll cooperate. I've had just about enough of your non-cooperation with the police, Mr. Stratton. The very least you can do now you've got the chance is to assist the police in their inquiries, but if you don't take that chance—"

"I'll take it," said Guy.

SIX

Leonard had just finished his lunch, which had consisted of a pint of beer and a slab of cheese on stale bread, when the telephone rang. The afternoon yawned emptily before him.

"Hullo?" he said hopefully into the receiver.

"Dad, it's me. Listen, what do you think's happened?

The police have been here off and on all morning, and they've just taken Guy off to Castlesea! He's not arrested but they hinted that unless he cooperated with them he would be. What do you make of that?"

"Christ," said Leonard, sitting down abruptly.

"Did the police come to the pub again this morning?"

"Yes, they arrived at eleven and told me all about the goings-on at Trecellan Hall."

"They must have seen you in between their visits to the Rectory. Dad, what do you think'll happen to Guy? They can't really have the evidence to arrest him, can they?"

"How the hell should I know?" Leonard ran a distracted hand through his hair. "Here, what about the girl? What about Jenny? Did she go with him?"

"No, she wanted to but he thought it would be best for her to stay at the Rectory. She's awfully upset—she's gone to her room. Grace thinks it would be better to leave her alone, but Mother isn't so sure."

"Put her on the phone."

"Who? Mother?"

"No, stupid. Jenny."

"I don't think she'll—"

"Do me a favor, would you? Just ask her. That's all. Just ask her if she'll come to the phone for a minute."

"Okay," said Ted, and Leonard heard the click as he put the receiver aside.

There was a pause. Leonard adjusted his position on the stool, crossed one leg over the other and regarded his shabby shoes with distaste.

"Hullo?" said Jenny, her voice sounding faraway and subdued.

"Hullo, love, sorry to hear about your troubles. Listen, I was thinking of taking my boat out for a couple of hours this afternoon. Why don't you come along with me? You don't want to be sitting around in your room wondering what's happening to Guy, and I don't suppose there'll be any news till this evening. I keep my boat at Porthmawgan on the estuary. Why don't I pick you up in my car in about half an hour?"

"Well, I . . . it's very kind of you—"

"Say you'll come, love. To please me."

"Well . . ."

"Okay?"

"All right. Thank you."

"See you in half an hour," said Leonard satisfied, and hung up.

SEVEN

"All right, Mr. Stratton," said Davies. "I think I have a clearer picture of your activities now."

They were still in Cellanporth. To his relief Guy had been taken not to the police headquarters in Castlesea but to the house of the village constable who had loaned Davies his front parlor. The Inspector paused to collect his thoughts. "You say that Emma made no mention of Charles' theory. She just asked you what you thought of Anne's accusation."

"Well, she may have been fishing for a hint that I was guilty of killing my first wife, but I was too damn angry that she'd tricked me into meeting her to pay attention."

"What did you say about that scene?"

"I brushed it off. I said something ridiculous like: 'Maybe Anne was right and Charles is a murderer—did you ever consider that?' And then I started to walk away."

"Hmm," said Davies. There was a pause as Guy wiped the sweat from his forehead. "It strikes me," said Davies carefully, "that your sister Anne is the key to the whole case. I know Dr. Carpenter says she can't be relied on as a witness, but I'm beginning to believe it was Anne's accusation that started the chain of events which led to Emma's murder. In fact, I'm almost sure that Anne witnessed your wife's death. The murderer's safe though because it looks as if Anne's credibility as a witness will be low for a long time. And, until the morning when she accused Charles St. Cellan, she'd given no indication that she remembered anything about your wife's death."

"That's true," said Guy heavily. "She often spoke of Christina as if Christina were trying to kill her but Roger says such statements are merely symptomatic of her illness."

"Hmm . . . you've consulted other doctors, of course, about yours sister's case?"

"Several specialists, yes, but there wasn't much they could do apart from prescribe drugs—and Roger can do that himself. In fact Roger's the only one who really seems to do her any good. All the other doctors seemed to upset her."

"I see. It's Dr. Carpenter, isn't it, who's always considered Anne's statements unreliable. And he's always taken a very special interest in your sister right from the beginning of her illness."

"Yes, he calls several times a week to see how she is."

"Very conscientious."

"Yes, he's very concerned about her."

"Hmm," said Davies for the third time and wandered over to the lace curtains to peer out into the street.

"Rhys, do you have the address and phone number of the people Charles St. Cellan is planning to stay with?"

"I think so, sir, yes." Rhys began to thumb through his notebook.

"He's lucky to have somewhere to go," said Guy dryly. "Most of his friends live in London. He doesn't even have to worry about having his wardrobe destroyed. He can always raid his Castlesea boutique for more of those unisex clothes he likes so much."

"Clothes," said Davies.

"Didn't you say all his clothes had been destroyed in the fire?"

"So I did," said Davies slowly. "So I did." He swung round on Rhys. "Get him on the phone for me, will you, please."

"Yes, sir."

"Why are you darting off at a tangent like this?" Guy demanded. "Why are you suddenly so interested in Charles? And why don't you arrest me and get it over with instead of keeping me hanging around like this?"

"I'd be very happy to arrest you after the way you've behaved," said Davies equably. "You had a good motive and a splendid opportunity for murdering both your wife and Emma St. Cellan, and by telling all those lies you've certainly acted the part of the murderer. But fortunately for you, I can't bring myself to believe you burned down Trecellan Hall. I'd like to believe it, but I don't. Very tiresome."

Guy swallowed. "Why?"

"You've got a very pretty wife and you haven't been married long. You'd have to be very drunk indeed not to make love to her when she obviously wanted you to so much."

Guy went scarlet.

"Too drunk to find an empty bottle, fill it with petrol, attach a nicely saturated wick and carry your brand new bomb over the Downs to Trecellan Hall. And too drunk to light the wick and fling the bottle with unerring accuracy clean through the middle of the windowpane."

The sergeant came back into the room. "I've got Mr. St. Cellan on the line, sir."

"Thanks, Rhys." Davies went into the hall and picked up the receiver. "Mr. St. Cellan? Inspector Davies. Listen, I want you to think back to that morning when you went to the Rectory and Anne Stratton accused you of murder. What were you wearing at the time?"

EIGHT

Leonard had a small light speedboat which bobbed up and down jauntily at its moorings. Climbing aboard, Jenny discovered a microscopic cabin where it was possible for one person to shelter from the elements, and a neat wheelhouse where the engine controls were situated. The sun shone; the water sparkled; in spite of herself Jenny began to feel better.

It had been a dreadful morning.

The first interview with the police had been bad enough, but the second interview, which had produced her own collapse followed by Guy's angry confession, had seemed the end of the world.

"I'll call you as soon as I get the opportunity," Guy had promised, and as if by repeating the words often enough he could make them come true, he had added: "It'll be all right. I know it's going to be all right."

"My dear," Marguerite had declared when the police had left, "I feel so dreadfully sorry for you—"

"Oh no you don't!" Jenny had cried, all her shock and anger surfacing at last. "You've never liked Guy and you don't like me and you're enjoying every minute of this! Don't you dare sympathize with me!" And before anyone could say another word she had burst into tears, rushed upstairs and locked herself in her bedroom.

She had cried for a long time, but to her relief no one had disturbed her. Later when she was more composed she had sat on the window seat and tried to think clearly, but she had still been too upset, and the more she had told herself Guy was certainly innocent the more convinced she had become of his guilt. In the end she had thought: no wonder the police believe him guilty—who else could they suspect if not Guy?

At that point she had become painfully aware that she still loved him no matter what he had done, and she had just begun to wonder desperately how she was going to endure the next few hours when Leonard had phoned with his invitation to join him on his boat. The idea of escaping from Marguerite and the Rectory had been irresistible. Now, as Leonard cast off and began to maneuver the boat down the estuary to the sea, she said thankfully, "It was clever of you to suggest this—I think I'd have gone mad if I'd had to stay at the Rectory all afternoon with everyone tiptoeing about and carrying on hushed conversations behind my back."

"Not much fun being pitied, is it, love? Here, have a seat—that's right. Are you warm enough? I know it's hot now but it'll be cooler once we get out to sea."

"I'm fine."

"Good. Now where would you like to go?"

Jenny sighed and stared at the familiar curve of the bay, the miles of sands, the steep slopes of the Downs. Far away lay the scarred cliffs of the Cellanporth headland and the black hump of the Snake's Tail.

"How about a trip to the old Tail?" suggested Leonard, following her glance. "There's a cove where we can land, and we can sit on the rocks there like a couple of mermaids while we drink the Coca-Cola I've got in the locker."

Jenny laughed. "I can't imagine you as a mermaid!"

"Seeing's believing," said Leonard and pulled out the throttle so that the boat surged forward into the salt waters of the bay.

Don't think of Guy, said a voice inside Jenny's head. Don't think of anything except the flying spray and the Snake's Tail in the distance and the exhilaration of swooping along in a speedboat. Think of the gulls and the surf and the way the light glints on the water. Think of Leonard's white sports shirt which reminds me of tennis players and those horrible baggy trousers which look as if they haven't been cleaned for years. Think of anything except murder and arson and Guy . . .

Guy. Meeting Emma, lying to the police, arrested in all but name . . .

"Perk up, love," said Leonard. "Have a cigarette."

"Thanks." She accepted one gratefully and began to fumble for her light.

"You'll never get a light out here in this breeze. Step into the cabin."

When she rejoined him the boat was heading straight for the horizon and the bay was receding before her eyes.

"I can't seem to escape from the Rectory," she said after a moment. "Wherever I go I can always see it. I can see it now. I could see it the other day when I walked out to the Snake's Tail with Ted. It's always there."

Leonard reduced his speed before altering course and steering southwest toward the long disjointed arm of the Cellanporth headland. "What did you and Ted find to talk about on your way to the Tail and back?"

"Oh . . ." Jenny tried to concentrate. "He talked about Anne. I think he's awfully in love with her."

"Poor kid," said Leonard. "Did he talk about Christina?"

"No. At least, not much. But Marguerite told me how Christina had—" She stopped.

"—slept with him?" said Leonard.

"Oh no!" said Jenny at once. "It was nothing like that, I'm sure . . ." Even as she spoke she was remembering Roger's assertion that Ted and not Christina had been the driving force behind the relationship. "I'm sure there was nothing serious between them," she said lamely.

"It was serious all right, love. They were having an affair, if you really want to know. And it wasn't Christina who made all the passes either," Leonard added, echoing Roger.

"You're quite certain—"

"Certain as can be, love. It's one of those cold hard facts of life, as I kept telling myself at the time. Guy and Christina come down here for a visit with their marriage

in tatters and all Christina can do is bitch about how
bloody boring Cellanporth is and then—bingo! Ted
comes home for a while and suddenly Christina thinks
Cellanporth is the loveliest most fascinating place on
earth. She hadn't seen Ted for over a year and we all
know how boys grow up. So there she is, all poised for a
splendid little diversion, and there's Ted, all poised to
fight his way clear of Marguerite's smother-love . . . well,
they couldn't miss, could they? But after Ted's grown up
about five years in five days he suddenly realizes that
Anne is much more his type than Christina and what's
even better, she's secretly crazy about him and she's been
suffering agonies while Christina's been dillydallying
around just to amuse herself. But that doesn't alter the
fact that he'd had an affair with Christina. I know that's
true beyond any shadow of a doubt."

"Did he tell you about it?"

"No, but Christina did." Leonard was looking placidly
out to sea. "She told me I was too old and drank too
much and Ted was one hell of a lot more fun . . . Now,
don't look like that! Not after we've both agreed how
lousy it is to have people tiptoeing around feeling sorry
for you! None of that matters any more anyway.
Christina died and Ted fell in love with Anne and I've got
my lady friend in Porthmawgan and everyone's happy as
a lark—except that Christina was probably murdered,
Anne's crazy and I'm getting very tired of my lady friend.
Sex is a nasty problem, isn't it, love? God, that Christina!
She was a piece all right. I was bloody upset when I found
out she had her talons into Ted. The night of the party
. . . well, never mind the night of the party. I tried to reason with her but she just laughed. That's when she said
what a lousy lover I was." He glanced at Jenny with a

grin. "She was dead wrong, of course, but . . . hey, am I embarrassing you? Well, never mind. You look lovely with pink cheeks. Most people when they blush go that horrible purple-red as if they're having heart failure . . . are you sure you're not cold, by the way? I've got an extra sweater in the cabin locker and you can borrow it if you like."

"Maybe I will," said Jenny in relief, and dived thankfully into the tiny cabin.

"On the left," called Leonard.

"Okay." She stopped to open the locker and pull out the sweater inside.

"Can you see it?" shouted Leonard. "It's that vile green thing with a white border which looks like a pattern from a Victorian lavatory. I never wear it unless I'm at least a mile out to sea."

Jenny stood motionless, the sweater in her hands. She went on standing motionless for ten full seconds, and then the sweater slipped from her fingers as her hands started to tremble.

NINE

"It was from the surplus stock at our boutique," said Charles. "There were two left and Emma wanted to get rid of them so I took one and she gave Leonard the other. It was rather a splendid shade of green—"

"Just a moment," interrupted Davies. "You say she gave one to Leonard."

"Yes, Leonard Matthews. The proprietor of the pub. You know. Old Leonard. He and Emma were quite chummy for a while. I say, what are you getting at?"

"Thank you, Mr. St. Cellan," said Davies, replacing the receiver, but as he stepped back into the parlor his first words to Rhys and Guy were, "We're off to the pub."

TEN

"I'm going to drop anchor here," said Leonard, cutting the engine. "Do you mind getting your feet wet? I don't want to go in any closer or the shingle will scratch the poor boat's bottom. Where are those bottles of Coke? Ah yes, here we are. Are you all right, love? You're looking as green as the sweater. You're not seasick, are you?"

"A bit." Jenny tried to smile but found her lips were curiously stiff.

"Okay, let's go ashore." He scrambled out of his shoes and socks and rolled up his trousers. "Would you like me to carry you?"

"Oh no. No, I'll be fine. I don't mind paddling. The water's not very deep, is it? I don't mind at all." Her voice sounded odd. She listened to it with a fascinated detachment and marveled at the rush of meaningless words which streamed from her lips. "Shall I carry one of the bottles?"

"No, that's all right, love. Everything's under control."

Jenny's thoughts turned and twisted frantically. She could take the speedboat out to sea again—except she had no idea how to start the engine. She could go ashore and hide. She could—

"Want a hand?" offered Leonard, turning to help her jump down into the water, and before she was aware of what was happening he was forcing her to jump. His fingers were thick and strong and muscular. She could imagine herself struggling against those fingers in vain . . .

"You know, love, you're not looking at all well." Leonard was staring at her with sharp-eyed concern. "What's up? You weren't really feeling seasick, were you? You're looking just as green now as you did on the boat."

He suspected. He could tell she was terrified. He would guess. He would look at the sweater and look at her and he would guess that she had seen Charles St. Cellan wearing an identical sweater the day Anne had called him a murderer . . . Christina's murderer. And once Leonard realized she knew—

"Leonard," she said. "Leonard, I think I want to go away somewhere and be quietly sick. It's a reaction to the news about Guy. I'm sorry, but I can't help it. Could you look the other way for a moment, please?"

"Of course. You poor little thing," he said sympathetically, and sat down on a rock with his back to her.

Jenny ran.

She scrambled up the slope from the cove, up the hump of the hillside which formed the spine of the Snake's Tail, and down the other side to the path which led from the end of the Tail toward the headland. She was dimly aware that there was no hiding place, but so great was her panic that the knowledge with all its appalling implications made no impact on her. She stared around blankly at the bare slopes of the peninsula with its short grass and patches of heather, stared at the scattered rocks which were all too small to conceal her, stared at the sea which slapped continuously at the low rocky cliffs before her. No beaches on this side of the Tail, no caves, no cover. That meant there was no choice. She would have to head for the mainland. She would have to run down the path to the causeway and begin that agonizingly slow scramble across the tortuous jumble of rocks which separated her from safety.

She started to run.

She was trying not to think of Leonard's muscular fingers and the surefooted speed he had displayed on leaving the boat. Despite his hint that he drank too much she guessed he was in good physical condition—good enough to outpace her once she reached the causeway.

There wasn't a second to lose.

She went on running. Her breath was coming in sobbing gasps and tears blinded her eyes. She tried to calculate how close she was to the causeway, hidden by the curving hump of the peninsula. Surely she couldn't be far away now. Once she rounded the bend of the path ahead of her the causeway would be visible, and the bend of the path was hardly more than a minute away. A minute.

She started to count. One. Two. Three . . .

She had to stop for five of those precious seconds to regain her breath. Her side was aching and suddenly she was so hot that she struggled out of the sweater and flung it to the ground. She had started to run again when she realized she would have to retrieve it unless she wanted to leave a signpost for Leonard, but then she thought: let him find it; it'll stop him for a minute and he's bound to guess anyway that I'm heading for the mainland.

Leonard.

She spun round in fear to see if there was any sign of him, but the landscape was empty, and sobbing with relief she started to run again. She was very near the bend in the path now. In ten seconds she would be able to see the causeway.

One, two, three . . .

Nearly there. Very nearly there.

Five, six, seven . . .

It was taking longer than she thought. The curve of the path was endless.

Eleven, twelve, thirteen . . . And she was there. The curve lay behind her at last, the ground was sloping down to sea level beneath her feet and there before her lay the causeway.

Except that it was no longer visible.

It was high tide. Above the causeway surf boiled in an endless droning roar, and littered like jagged black teeth in this swirling inferno were the tallest of the causeway rocks, all that now remained visible of her escape route to the mainland.

ONE

There was nowhere to hide.

Jenny stumbled down to the water's edge but she was afraid of being swept off her feet by one of the large waves which were cresting violently through the channel of water. For a second she thought she might squeeze be-

neath the overhanging bank, but if Leonard were to follow her to the water's edge he would see her at once.

Leonard.

She whirled around again in terror, fully expecting to
see him emerging from the long curve of the path, but
there was still no sign of him. How long would it be before he reached the curve? By now he must surely be
looking for her.

A large wave burst on a nearby rock; spray, cold and
harsh, slapped her in the face, and suddenly her panic
was under control and her mind, fogged by fear, became
sharp and decisive. If Leonard were now on the path
which led along the southern side of the peninsula, she
must take care to be on the northern side so that the con-
cealing hump of the peninsula's backbone was between
them. Moving rapidly she left the shingle by the edge of
the water, clawed her way up the bank and stumbled
through the short grass which clung to the hump's northern slopes.

As soon as she was safely away from the water she
stopped and glanced up the steep slope to her left. An irresistible urge to discover where Leonard was overcame
her. Scrambling up the hillside she dropped onto her
hands and knees and crawled the last few feet to the sum-
mit of the ridge.

She looked down to the path below.

He was there. As her heart thumped painfully against
her ribs she pressed her face to the ground, but when she
dared to look again she saw that she was safe; he had not
seen her. He had reached the discarded sweater, and as
she watched he stopped to pick it up. The next moment
he was looking around him swiftly but she had anticipated
this and was already pressing her face to the ground

again. The next time she raised her head she saw that
he was still standing with the sweater in his hands, but
now he was staring at the waves breaking against the
shallow cliffs below the path.

He stared at the sea for a long time. At last he picked
his way carefully through the heather to the edge of the
cliffs, but there was nothing to be seen there, and presently he returned to the path again, tied the sweater
around his waist and set off at first slowly and then with
increasing speed in the direction of his boat.

Jenny stayed exactly where she was on top of the ridge.
The wind scudded in from the sea to chill her to the bone,
and then as she began to shiver uncontrollably she saw
the little speedboat hum away from its harbor on the
northern side of the peninsula and hurtle across the bay
to Porthmawgan.

She watched it recede into the distance. When at last
the boat was a mere fleck of white on the blue waters of
the bay she dragged herself behind a rock which offered
shelter from the wind, collapsed in a heap amidst the
coarse heather and began to sob with the enormity of her
relief.

TWO

When Leonard reached Porthmawgan he immediately
shut himself in the nearest public call box and telephoned
the Rectory-by-the-Sea. His son answered the phone on
the fourth ring.

"Ted? It's me. Listen, I'm in a bloody awful jam. I've
lost Jenny. Yes lost—L-O-S-T. I know it's fantastic but

I've done it. I'm going to call the police and organize a search party but I thought I'd call the Rectory first to see if by any chance Guy was there."

"No, there's been no word about Guy at all. But Dad, how on earth—"

"I don't know—I just can't think what can have happened, but I'm scared stiff she's fallen into the sea and drowned."

"You're not serious!"

"Serious! I'm bloody hysterical. I took her out for a spin in the boat and we landed on the Tail to have a picnic and suddenly she's as green as her sweater—you know, that godawful one Emma gave me—and says she's going off to be sick. So I turn my back politely and wait and wait and wait and nothing happens—no Jenny—nothing—"

"You mean she disappeared?"

"Into thin air!"

"But why?"

"Who cares why? It's how she disappeared that gives me the creeps. You know the Tail—no cover anywhere, just the odd rock or two. Well, I looked and looked for her but all I found was her sweater—the one I lent her—lying on the ground on the south side above those shallow cliffs. My God, if she had an accident, slipped, drowned—or supposing she was so upset about Guy that she deliberately—"

"Oh listen, Dad, she can't have done! She must have cut across the causeway to the mainland—"

"It was high tide! No, she must have had an accident and drowned herself—there's no other explanation. Listen, Ted, while I get a search party organized could you go over to the Tail and have another look for her? The tide was on the turn when I left and by the time you get out there the causeway should be passable again—"

"I'm on my way. Incidentally, Dad—"

"Yes?"

"The police are waiting at the pub for you."

"What the hell for?"

"I don't know. They called in at the Rectory, but I didn't tell them you'd gone out in the boat so they decided to go back to the pub to wait for you to come back."

"Why didn't you tell them where I was, for God's sake?"

"I don't know." Ted sounded mutinous. "I don't like policemen and I didn't feel in a cooperative mood."

"What's the trouble?"

"I drove out to Porthmawgan to see Anne but the matron wouldn't let me in. That so-and-so Roger Carpenter has been playing God again . . . Okay, I'm off to the Tail. See you later."

"Thanks a million," said Leonard and hung up.

It took him thirty-five minutes of breakneck driving to reach the pub. The police car was parked at the door and as he drew up he saw the inspector and the sergeant emerge from the front seat to greet him. He was so preoccupied that he did not notice Guy sitting in the back.

"Mr. Matthews," Davies began, "I wonder if we could—"

"Look," said Leonard rapidly, "this is an emergency—could you get some more coppers to help search the Snake's Tail? I took Jenny Stratton there this afternoon and I can't find her and I think she must have had an accident. I don't know how it could have happened but . . ."

"We'll find her, Mr. Matthews, but first we have to ask you one or two more questions."

"Later—okay?" Leonard's patience was wearing thin. "I'm going to ring up some local men and get them to come out to the Tail with me. I can't waste time talking to you when—"

"I'm afraid you'll have to, Mr. Matthews," said Davies, motioning Guy to stay where he was. "But we needn't sit down—we can all stand right here. You were at the St. Cellans' party the night she died, weren't you? What were you wearing at the time?"

Leonard, forgetting Jenny for a moment, gave him a look of incredulous amazement. "What was I wearing? For Christ's sake! I can't remember. Sweater and slacks, I expect. Why?"

"Can you describe the sweater for us?"

"Can I—look, what *is* this?"

"Just answer the question, if you don't mind, Mr. Matthews. What color was the sweater?"

"Well, it was either my dishwater beige or my funeral blue. I don't have any others."

"What about your green sweater with the white trimming at the neck and cuffs?"

"Oh that!" said Leonard scornfully. "I wouldn't be seen dead in that! The only time I ever wear it is when I'm well out to sea in my boat." And then as a thought struck him: "How the hell did you know about that sweater?"

"So you deny wearing it to the St. Cellans' party. You're quite sure you're not mistaken?"

"Look, I wouldn't wear that sweater to anyone's party, not even the St. Cellans'. And besides—" Memory returned to him suddenly "—I know for a fact I couldn't have worn it that night. It was out on loan at the time."

There was a small still pause. Leonard felt a pang of fear. "Here, what *is* all this? What's it all about? Why all this fuss about that godawful sweater?"

But all Davies said was, "Who did you loan the sweater to, Mr. Matthews?" and Leonard found himself answering in a faltering voice which did not sound like his at all: "There was a cold wind that afternoon, you see—we'd had lunch together at the pub, and the wind blew up from the southwest afterwards—I didn't keep the sweater on my boat then, and when he left I lent him the sweater for the walk home."

"You mean you lent it to—"

"My son," said Leonard. He felt stupefied by fear. "I lent it to my son . . ."

THREE

Jenny saw Ted far off on the other side of the causeway as she was walking down to the water's edge to see how far the tide had receded. She was still feeling lightheaded with relief, and when she saw Ted she waved to him and began scrambling across the slippery rocks of the causeway.

She soon discovered that progress was going to be wet as well as slow. The tide was still high and occasionally a large wave would have enough strength to wash across the rocks and soak her slacks to the knee. Seaweed made the rocks treacherous even to her rubber-soled shoes and twice she slipped, once skinning her elbow and the second time tearing her slacks at the thigh. But the knowledge that she was alive and safe made her careless of such minor discomforts. She clambered on doggedly, only pausing now and then to push the hair from her eyes and see how much closer Ted was.

He too was moving quickly. His breathing had fallen into a swift economical rhythm, every muscle in his body was coordinating smoothly, each footstep was deft and sure. Everything was under control; the sea couldn't catch him, nobody could catch him; there would just be Jenny all alone among that jumble of black rocks in the middle of the causeway and she wouldn't suspect anything until it was too late.

Jenny suspected Leonard. She had seen the sweater, and because she knew it belonged to Leonard she had immediately assumed he was the murderer. That was obvious from Leonard's story. "She turned green as her sweater—you know, the sweater Emma gave me . . ." Jenny had seen the sweater, recognized it as being identical to the one Charles St. Cellan had worn that morning when Anne had accused him of murder. Ted had thought that only he, Emma and Anne had actually seen Charles that morning, but Jenny had obviously seen him too and had somehow managed to link Anne's fearful identification to the sweaters from Emma's Boutique . . .

Everything had gone wrong after that scene at the Rectory.

For a whole year, ever since Christina's death, he had thought he was safe. Anne had remembered nothing, and he was almost sure anyway that she hadn't seen him properly in the darkness. The inquest had produced a verdict of accidental death. If people suspected foul play their suspicions had fallen on Anne, and Anne was safe because Roger Carpenter would have insisted with his dying breath that Anne was unfit to plead or, even if she were fit, that she had not been responsible for her actions.

Everything had been fine, better than he had dared to hope.

And then out of the blue had come Anne's false but appallingly dangerous accusation.

He had known at once that he was in great trouble. Supposing Anne remembered more; supposing she eventually realized he was the murderer? But he couldn't bring himself to believe that Anne would ever be a danger to him. She loved him and he loved her. If she remembered she might tell him but she would never tell anyone else. Meanwhile she was confused and he had to cope with the results of her confusion.

After a moment of panic he had decided that if he were lucky the incident would be dismissed and eventually forgotten. So long as no one knew—or remembered—what Charles had been wearing at the time, he would be safe.

But he had watched Emma closely. Emma was sharp and there was always the possibility that she would put two and two together. When she had come into the pub that night and admitted to Leonard that she had a rendezvous later, Ted had immediately been suspicious. As soon as he was alone he had run upstairs and seen Emma and Guy as they returned from the headland.

Emma and Guy. He could picture the scene clearly, picture Emma saying: "There's only one explanation for Anne's odd behavior—she remembered the sweater. It's identical to the one I gave Leonard. What do you think? Should we tell the police?" And once the police learned

Ted had borrowed the sweater, they would know he had killed Christina.

He had gone downstairs again just as Emma had come into the pub. He had asked her about Guy at once, but she had just laughed and told him to mind his own business. When he had gone on asking her she finally said irritated, "I was trying to find out what Guy thought about Anne calling Charles a murderer. I told Guy I met him for a bet but actually Charles and I had our suspicions about who Anne thought Charles was and I couldn't resist the opportunity of finding out if Guy would give himself away."

Ted hadn't heard the last part of the sentence. He had stopped listening after she had said: "We had our suspicions about who Anne thought Charles was . . ." He had stopped listening, stopped breathing, stopped thinking—until Emma had said suddenly: "Hey, what's the matter with you? Why are you looking at me like that?" And after he had shaken his head violently and muttered some meaningless explanation she had said suddenly, "The sweaters. Charles was wearing the sweater I gave to Len. It was Len, wasn't it? My God, and you knew! No wonder you looked like that! It was your own father!" And all Ted could think was that once the police suspected Leonard everything would be discovered. Leonard would have lied for him, but he wouldn't have known until too late how important it was to lie . . .

After Emma's death Ted had hunted for the sweater but had finally decided Leonard had thrown it away. So Emma was dead, Leonard's sweater had disappeared but surely it would be only a matter of time before Charles realized the terrible significance of the sweater. It was impossible to think of killing Charles who kept a gun at the Hall and was obviously prepared for an attack from the murderer. But if a fire destroyed all Charles' clothes . . .

After the fire Ted had convinced himself once again that he was safe. Both sweaters were gone—or so he thought —and Charles, obsessed with his conviction that Guy was guilty, had none of his sister's intuition and intelligence. And then had come Leonard's revelation not only that he kept his sweater on his boat but that Jenny had seen the sweater and linked it to Anne's accusation.

Of all the people in Cellanporth Jenny had seemed the least likely to prove dangerous to him.

But Jenny had become dangerous. And Jenny was now only fifty yards away from him across the rocks.

He waved to her again, called out "Hi!" but his greeting was drowned by the roar of the water.

It would be easy to kill her. The rocks were slippery, the larger waves were still breaking across the low-lying ground and the sea was erratic and turbulent. He could almost hear himself talking about it afterwards to the police. She tried to cross the causeway too soon. There was this great wave which knocked her off her feet. She hit her head on a rock . . . lost consciousness . . . sucked out to sea with the undertow . . . tried to save her, but he'd been too far away.

Easy.

Christina had been easy to kill too, perhaps because it had been an accident. He had lashed out at her blindly and she had slipped, lost her balance, fallen . . . He could see her rolling over and over down the steep slope, her mouth wide open, her eyes bright with terror, her hands scrabbling at the coarse grass which clung to the edge of the cliff . . .

With Emma it was harder. After she had remembered the sweater that night in the pub he had managed after a short but terrible struggle to knock her unconscious; then he had carried her outside and rolled her body deliberately over the cliff. His scalp still prickled with fright at the thought of it. But what else could he have done? It was easy afterwards to say that she'd never been back to the pub. Horrible but easy.

Killing Jenny would be the same. All he had to do was to blot any feeling from his mind and concentrate on one thing at a time. The next rock, the next crashing breaker, the next swirl of ice-cold water inches from his sandals ...

"Hi Jenny!" he called again.

"Hi!" He could hear her now. Three more rocks to scramble across and she would be face to face with him.

"Are you okay?" he heard himself say breathlessly as he drew level with her.

"Yes . . . my God, am I glad to see you!" She was crying. "Ted, I've been so scared. I found a sweater of your father's and I know Charles had one just like it. He was wearing it when Anne said he was a murderer—"

Curiosity made him interrupt. "So you saw Charles then? I thought you said you didn't."

"I know—I was flustered because I'd been eavesdropping and I wanted you to think I'd been in my room. I was on my way upstairs to tell Emma Charles had arrived when Anne made that awful remark. After that I somehow didn't like to join you, so I—" She stopped.

"Yes?"

She was staring at him. "You were in the room. You must have seen the sweater too. You must have realized—" She stopped again.

"I had to protect my father," he said woodenly.

But she was looking at him very oddly, just as Emma had looked at him that night in the pub. Had he given himself away again? He didn't see how he could have done, and yet she was looking at him in that puzzled, fearful way . . .

"Why are you staring at me like that?" But it was not his voice asking the question. It was hers.

She took a pace backwards, slipped on the rock and flung out a hand to steady herself. Her face was very pale. The freckles on the bridge of her nose were like small stark smudges on the chalky whiteness of her skin.

"It was you, wasn't it?" she said at last. "It wasn't Leonard, it was you who killed Christina."

"It was an accident." His voice sounded different, world-wise and mature. "You see, she was trying to kill Anne. She was jealous of Anne because I loved Anne and I told Christina that I didn't want to sleep with her any more. But Christina wouldn't take no for an answer. She made scenes, tried to cling to me . . . it was disgusting. I can't think what I ever saw in her. As soon as I knew I was in love with Anne, Christina just seemed old and stupid and even a bit pathetic, drinking too much and taking all those filthy drugs . . . I didn't want her any more. She was crazy—she tried to kill Anne by slipping her LSD in the car and then taking her out along the headland to the edge of the cliffs. I got there just in time. I always claimed afterwards that I stayed at the pub but I didn't. Christina turned round when she heard me coming. She said, 'Keep away from her—she's on a bum trip. I let her drop some acid a while ago and now she's trying to push me over the cliff.' But then she grabbed at Anne and I saw it was just the other way round—that Anne was the one in danger—

and I lashed out at Christina . . . Anne ran away. I tried to follow her but she disappeared. I thought she'd gone back to the Rectory but she never came back . . . never . . . It's been a terrible punishment for me. I killed to save her from death and yet now it's worse than if she really was dead."

"But Emma—that couldn't have been an accident—"

"No, I had to kill her because she was like you—she guessed. The thing that upset me most afterwards was that people might suspect Anne again. . . . I tell you, I've been through hell. And if Emma had given the game away it would have meant that I'd suffered all those months for nothing, don't you see? I couldn't have stood that. I didn't want to kill her, but I had to . . . I don't want to kill you either but I have to, I just have to . . ." He was crying suddenly. He didn't know why. His mind was blank but he was still aware of a massive weariness blotting out his self-control.

She touched him. She put her hand on his arm and said in a soft gentle voice, "Poor Ted. What a terrible burden it must have been for you. But you don't have to carry it around any longer. There are lots of people who can help you. We can all help you. If we go back now together—"

He had to kill her then because if he had listened to her for a second longer he would have been unable to touch a hair of her head. Her hand was still on his arm. With a jerk he seized her wrist, forced her to the ground and slid his hands around her throat before she even had time to scream.

An enormous wave burst like a thunderclap behind him. Water swept over Jenny, washing her away from him and knocking him off his feet. He staggered, slipped, fell. He was still struggling to his feet seconds later when a hand reached out to grab him and spinning round incredulously he found himself face to face with Davies.

He had one last coherent thought: Not that.

Another wave broke over them. He could feel Davies' grip loosen and in a flash his reflexes had wrenched him free. Not thinking, not hesitating, not even conscious of fear, he slid on all fours down the sloping slimy shelf of rock and fought his way through the boiling surf to the clear calm welcoming waters beyond.

FOUR

The surf was dragging Jenny down, pressing on her eyelids, filling her mouth, streaming through her hair. All she was conscious of was the noise, the roar of the undertow dragging the water over a million pebbles. She was hurled against a rock but there was no time to cry out and almost no time to feel pain. She felt beyond everything except the desire to stop the roar of the sea as it strove to batter her to pulp. Another wave pulled her in a different direction; she clawed at a rock but it slipped past her fingers. Making a last wild effort to save herself she reached out again and this time she was luckier. Her fingers closed around something slim and strong. Incredulously she realized she was clinging to a man's wrist, and a familiar voice was gasping her name.

It was Guy. Impossible, because Guy was at the police headquarters. She was imagining it, hallucinating before she drowned.

"Hang on, can you hear?" Guy was shouting, trying to pitch his voice above the roar of the surf. "Don't let go."

She hung on. Another wave broke over her head, Guy's fingers gave her a violent tug and suddenly she found herself lying on a high rock with all the water draining away from her into a gully below.

"Jenny?"

Guy was bending over her and his breath was coming in great gulps.

"Jenny!"

"Yes," she said. "Yes." She reached out to cling to him and he held her very tightly for a long moment. It was only when she opened her eyes again that she saw the policemen scrambling over the rocks some way away. They moved awkwardly, like puppets, around the water's edge as if they were looking for something.

"Guy—"

"Yes, I'm here. It's all right, darling. It's all right now."

"It was Ted—"

"Yes. We found out just in time. We saw Ted pass the pub on his way out here, but we didn't suspect anything —it wasn't until Leonard arrived ten minutes later that we realized . . . My God, those ten minutes! They were just enough to give Ted a good start on us. I'll never forget going down the path to the causeway—seeing you both meet . . . I thought we'd never get to you in time. I thought I was going to see you killed before my eyes. We shouted and shouted at him but the sea was so loud he never heard. Christ, if anything had happened to you . . ."

But Jenny was no longer listening. Tears were burning her cheeks. For a long time she was silent but when at last she could speak again all she said was, "Poor Leonard."

FIVE

Leonard closed the pub that night, locked himself in his kitchen with a bottle of whiskey and only roused himself sufficiently at eight the next morning to stagger to the bar for a second bottle. He was just pouring himself some breakfast when there was a brisk knock on the back door.

"Go 'way!" he yelled.

The knocking persisted. Growling he levered himself to his feet and somehow managed to open the back door.

Facing him was Grace Reid. "Good morning," she said, very competent and professional. "If you don't mind me saying so you look in great need of some medical care and attention. I've brought you a pint of milk and if you'll let me in I'll make you some tea."

"I don't need a nurse!" shouted Leonard.

"Rubbish," said Grace, stepping neatly past him into the kitchen and picking up the kettle. "This is the one time in your life when you need someone looking after you. Although I must say," she added, glancing dispassionately around the kitchen, "it looks as if you need permanent help. This place is a pigsty."

"I don't need anyone!" cried Leonard, quivering with rage.

"Very unconvincing," said Grace and dropped two fizzling tablets into a glass of water. "Drink this."

"Shan't," said Leonard.

"You're being very childish. Drink it up at once."

"Bloody interfering woman! Go away!"

"All right," said Grace. "Wallow in your self-pity all by yourself. I don't give a damn."

"Here! Where are you going?"

"You told me to go, didn't you? Well, I'm going. I detest loudmouthed self-centered men."

"Now wait a minute," said Leonard. "Don't get shirty. Wait a minute."

Grace stood poised on the threshold.

"If I drink this filthy liquid you've given me will you make some tea?"

"All right," said Grace. "And if I'm staying I suppose I might as well get you something to eat too. Is it too much to hope that you have anything edible in that horrid little refrigerator you keep under the television set?"

"There's bacon and eggs," said Leonard morosely. "And there's nothing wrong with that refrigerator, I'll have you know."

"I bet the bacon's green," said Grace.

But it wasn't. It crackled briskly in the frying pan ~~d presently Leonard's mouth began to water and he forgot the bottle of whiskey at his elbow.

"Are you going to have some too?" he said, watching her greedily as she broke the eggs into a bowl.

"That's an idea," said Grace, and broke two extra eggs without batting an eyelid.

Later as he sat facing her across the table Leonard said with gloomy interest, "You're a funny sort of character, aren't you?"

"That," said Grace dryly, "makes two of us."

There was a silence. For a long moment Leonard stared somberly at his plate, but as Grace held her breath he looked up at her across the table and somehow managed to smile.

SIX

"I shall go away," said Marguerite red-eyed, lying back on her pillows and reaching for a fresh handkerchief. "I shall get rid of this horrible house and never come back. I shall go on a cruise . . . round the world if possible, and when I come back . . . perhaps a little flat in London . . . somewhere quite different . . ."

"An excellent idea," murmured Roger soothingly. He finished writing the prescription for sedatives and placed it on the bedside table. "Much the best thing you could do."

She smiled at him wanly. She looked curiously vulnerable without the protective shield of her makeup, and suddenly he felt sorry enough for her to wish he could like her more than he did.

"Try and get as much rest as possible," he said to her kindly, turning toward the door. "I'll look in again tomorrow." And then he was running downstairs and out into the yard to his car.

It was time at last to go to the nursing home at Porthmawgan and visit Anne.

SEVEN

"Ted was drowned?" said Anne, more puzzled than upset now that the initial impact of the shock had passed. He had told her as gently as possible, but to his surprise and relief she had taken the news well. She had cried, but her tears had seemed like a miracle to him; he had half expected the news to send her into a further withdrawal, feared that she would not speak or show any emotion for days. But she had cried, cried as she never had before, until at last the tears had stopped and she was saying in a faltering voice that she had loved Ted so much even though seeing him had always reminded her of that night when the sea had been like molten gold. "He loved the sea," she said tearfully. "It couldn't have killed him. He loved it so much."

"He chose it, Anne. The police had discovered that he killed Christina."

"But Christina tried to kill me. I remember that—in fact now I can see it quite clearly. She tried to push me over the cliff."

"Do you remember Ted intervening?"

"Sort of." Anne frowned. Her eyes had an inward look. "No, not really. At least, I think I can remember a man pulling Christina away from me . . . I'm not sure." She clenched her fists tightly. "All I can really remember are the colors," she said at last. "It was night but everything was bright as day. The sea was gold and the sky was like purple velvet. Christina's hair shone like gold too and her skin was silver like a dead fish. She was trying to push me—" Anne shuddered convulsively.

"Don't go on if you don't want to."

"No, it's all right. I want to talk about it now because I can see it all so clearly. I didn't dare see it clearly before —I was frightened in case . . . well, I was so confused— for a while I thought *I'd* killed her. But I couldn't bear that so it was easier to believe that she was still alive. Sometimes I knew I hadn't killed her but somehow I didn't want to know who had. I still have no actual memory of Ted. But I can see that glittering flash of green, a brilliant green bordered by a dazzling gleaming white—the colors of that sweater. Charles St. Cellan wore that sweater. As soon as I saw him wearing it I felt sure it was he who had killed Christina and I was so relieved because I didn't mind him being a murderer. I jumped up and said, 'That's him! He's the murderer!' only no one believed me and after a while I didn't believe it either. Then I became afraid again and tried to blot it all from my mind—"

"Poor Anne."

"No, I'm all right." She glanced around at her clean neat little room. "I like it here. They like it too and there's always someone nearby if They start to frighten me."

"But you don't want to stay here too long, do you? I was thinking that if you felt better I might perhaps take you away somewhere and—"

"Oh no." She shook her head violently. "I don't want to go away. I like it here. I feel safe."

"But I could look after you—make you feel safe—"

"Ted used to say that." Her eyes filled with tears again. "I shall miss Ted so much." And as she covered her face with her hands he leaned forward and put an arm clumsily around her shoulders.

EIGHT

"By the way," said Guy to Jenny, "there's something I have to talk to you about."

Jenny looked at him in alarm. "What's that?" she said guiltily, assuming at once that she had made some embarrassing faux pas. "What have I done?"

They were in the living room at the Rectory. Beyond the window the sands stretched to the sea and beyond the sea a large subdued red sun had just disappeared behind the clear-cut line of the horizon.

"You've done nothing!" exclaimed Guy, smiling at her. "I'm the one who has the confession to make! Jenny, a few months ago I borrowed money from Roger and the other day I paid it back from our joint account. Now, I know that was essentially your money but I'm planning to pay it back out of my salary. I've got it all worked out. It'll take me about ten months, but—"

"Oh, for heaven's sake!" After being almost murdered and then nearly drowned Jenny was hardly prepared to be upset over minor financial problems. Besides, Guy had saved her life and she felt ashamed that she had ever suspected him of marrying her solely for her money. "Guy, we don't have to talk about that now, do we?"

"It's important to me," he said stiffly. "I wanted you to know that I plan to repay the money."

He was so awkward, so very unlike himself, that she felt alarmed again. "I'm sorry," she said uneasily. "Yes, of course it's important. But Guy, you don't have to repay the money—"

"I must," he said.

"But—"

"You must allow me some self-respect."

There was a silence. At last he said, "I should have told you about Roger's loan, but I was too proud—I didn't want you to know what a mess I'd made of my financial affairs."

"I understand." Jenny was acutely aware of her fortune lying between them like some unspeakable monster. Taking a deep breath she said, "Guy, you can't ignore the money. It's there. It's ours. We're very lucky and if we're going to spend all our time feeling guilty about it we'd be very stupid. I'm not saying we should waste it, but why can't we invest at least some if it in our future? Your career, for instance. I know you hate being an industrial architect and that you only went into that field because you needed the money. Wouldn't it be better now if you went into business on your own, and designed houses for people instead of skyscrapers for corporations? You'd be happier, and that would mean I'd be happier too. Why don't you start by designing a house for us? You know we don't want to live forever in a London flat."

He still looked troubled. After a moment he said uncertainly, "I'd have to think about it."

She leaned forward and kissed him. "What shall we call our house when it's built?"

"Stratton's Folly would be appropriate," he said gloomily, but the next moment he was laughing too, and beyond the window the stars were beginning to shine in the pale night sky.